APPROACHING OMEGA

APPROACHING OMEGA
Eric Brown

First published in England in 2005 by

Telos Publishing Ltd
61 Elgar Avenue, Tolworth, Surrey, KT5 9JP, England
www.telos.co.uk

Telos Publishing Ltd values feedback. Please e-mail us with
any comments you may have about this book to:
feedback@telos.co.uk

ISBN: 1-903889-98-7 (paperback)
Approaching Omega © 2005 Eric Brown.

ISBN: 1-903889-99-9 (hardback)
Approaching Omega © 2005 Eric Brown.

Printed in India

1 2 3 4 5 6 7 8 9 10 11 12 13 14 15

British Library Cataloguing in Publication Data.
A catalogue record for this book is available from the British
Library.

To Tony Ballantyne, Barbara, Robin and Michael.

Prelude

Latimer was awoken early by a blood-red sunrise, all the more beautiful for being the last on Earth he would ever witness. He slipped quickly from the bed, leaving Caroline asleep, showered and dressed and moved through the dome to the lounge.

He stood beneath the transparent arc of the wall and stared out across the greensward to the shimmering sea and the rising sun. It was as if the planet had conspired to produce a magnificent valedictory symbol, all the more poignant for being one of the few things of beauty in a slowly dying world.

He was lucky, he told himself; he was one of only five thousand human beings selected to leave the planet, push out to the stars, initiate Homo Sapiens' next stage of evolution light years away from where it all started. He had known for almost ten years now that he would be leaving, but it was as if before now the knowledge had been intellectual, an abstraction he found hard to believe: this morning, the morning of his last day on his home planet, it came to him in a dizzy rush that everything he experienced in the next few hours, he would never experience again. His last awakening

7

on Earth; his last appreciation of a Vancouver sunrise; his last breakfast with Caroline.

And later, at noon, he would have to attend the farewell event, and see his father, and his sister and her kids, for the very last time.

How do you say goodbye to loved ones when you know – and they know – that you will never meet again?

He pushed the thought to the back of his mind and touched the sensor pad on the holo-set.

He sat on the padded seat beneath the curve of the dome and watched the newscast. A reporter stood in the centre of the dome, as seemingly solid as himself, surrounded by an image of some war-torn African state. He killed the volume, so that she was miming silently to herself. He flipped channels. A reporter strolled along a desiccated river-bed, his mute, earnest gestures an eloquent testament to humankind's folly. Yet another channel showed a packed hospital ward in some South American country, beds full of the victims of the latest super-plague.

Latimer closed his eyes and not for the first time experienced, alongside the relief that he was leaving all this behind, a powerful wave of guilt.

He was leaving the world to choke on its own effluent. How long might civilisation last, at the butt end of the twenty-first century? How many more millions would die over the course of the next few years, while he lay in cold sleep, oblivious to everything? He had said farewell to friends and acquaintances, and that had been difficult enough – not so much facing the fact that he would never see these good people again, but having to recognise in their eyes, in their subtle body language, the very real, if unstated, resentment that he was escaping. That had been hard. He'd felt as though he were consigning these people to death sentences. He knew this was absurd, but at the same time he realised that when he first awoke, to maintain the ship fifteen hundred years into the voyage, his family and everyone else he knew – in fact everyone now alive on Earth – would be long dead.

Thank Christ, he thought, he would have Caroline.

He was about to kill the holo-set when the story changed: no longer scenes of food riots in Milan, but a sweeping aerial shot of a sloping greensward dotted with domes beside a small shuttle port: the Omega Corporation headquarters here in Vancouver.

The camera dropped to a reporter standing on a stretch of grass with the ocean in the background. Latimer had the odd experience of being able to see, in the middle-ground behind the woman, the dew-drop hemisphere of his own dome.

He turned up the sound. The woman was saying: "... historic day for planet Earth. In less than six hours, the four-person maintenance crew and the last of the colonists of the starship *Dauntless* will leave from this port and dock with the ship in orbit around planet Earth. According to the schedule, just five hours after this, the *Dauntless* will blast off for the stars. I have with me Mission Controller Sabine Courvier. Sabine, what are your feelings at this precise moment ...?"

The shot pulled back to show the petite, black-suited Omega Corporation executive. Latimer killed the sound before Courvier could respond with bland platitudes of her own.

The interview was soon over, replaced with orbital views of the *Dauntless*, its bull-nosed front-end trailing an attenuated superstructure upon which the five great cold sleep hangars were arranged like the spots on a die.

The scene changed again, cutting to the protestors encamped by the side of the road leading to the Omega Corporation's HQ.

Latimer upped the sound.

A reporter stood before a barrier, behind which a crowd of anti-colonisation demonstrators waved banners and chanted.

"As you can hear," the reporter shouted above the noise, "the anti-col lobby are making their protests heard here today. With me is Gerald Proxmire, spokesman for Earth First, one of the many protest groups opposed to the colonisation of the stars. Mr Proxmire, what is your main objection to the *Dauntless* mission?"

"Quite apart from the many billions spent on this quite reckless and privileged jaunt to the stars," Proxmire began, "billions which could have been spent on improving the lot of those of us who will remain on Earth –"

Latimer cut the broadcast and sat in the silence of the dome.

He'd heard their arguments many times before, of course, and dismissed them as specious: the bleatings of the envious who wished that they too could begin a new life among the stars. If the authorities had listened to the nay-sayers down the ages, opposed to every scientific and technological innovation, then humankind would still be living in caves.

He dismissed the small voice at the back of his mind which whispered that, perhaps, the funds could have been spent on improving things on the ravaged planet they were leaving.

He felt a soft touch on the back of his neck. "You're miles away, Ted."

He smiled up at Caroline, and felt a stomach-turning surge of affection for the woman who had been his wife for the past two years.

"Let's eat," she said in her soft, English tones.

He followed her out to the patio, where Omega staff had already set the table for breakfast.

10

It had been her voice, that cut-glass pronunciation and elegantly precise diction, that had been one of the many things that had attracted him to Caroline when they'd first met during routine training five years earlier.

She was small, fair, winsomely lovely. A strange combination of her obvious knowledge and learning, and her diffidence, had tugged at something within him.

Her specialisms were history – she had lectured at Cambridge before applying for the mission – and genetics: two disciplines seemingly poles apart, but which, she had argued, were inextricably linked, one encompassing the past and the other spanning not only ages long gone but all the times to come.

They had joked, in the early days of their relationship, that their love would last for centuries – and that had been before the final colonist selection had been made. Seven thousand men and women had trained for the mission, but only five thousand had made the final cut. He'd often asked himself what he would have done if Caroline had been rejected.

He would have resigned his commission, foregone the stars, and made a life on Earth with Caroline Stewart.

But now their love really would span centuries, millennia even.

They drank orange juice and ate croissants in the warming sunlight.

At one point she reached across the table and touched his hand. "Real yet?"

He smiled. "It won't be until we board the *Dauntless*, and maybe not even then. Maybe when I wake up in fifteen hundred years, for the first maintenance shift … maybe then it'll hit me what I've done." He grinned. "I'll miss you."

Caroline laughed. "We haven't been apart for more than a day before now."

"How will I survive fifteen centuries!"

She squeezed his fingers. "Only … what, subjectively? A few days for every fifteen hundred years, with estimated landfall within twenty thousand years … That's only a parting of a few weeks, real-time."

"Maybe I'll survive, then," he smiled.

The previous night they had watched the sun set – their very last sunset – and then watched the stars come out, and they had pointed at that section of the heavens into which they would be flying. Caroline identified the constellations of Canes Venatici and Ursa Major, and carolled the names of the beautiful stars: Alioth, Merak and Dubhe, any of which might harbour suitable, Earth-like planets.

Now Caroline said: "When we do find a planet, Ted, beautiful and unspoilt, we'll start a family, okay? I want a daughter." She was silent for a time, then said, in a soft voice: "We're so incredibly lucky. Sometimes I can't bring myself to believe what's happening to us."

His reply was interrupted by the chime of his communicator. He unclipped it from his belt. "Latimer," he said, annoyed at having his free time invaded.

An unfamiliar man's face stared out of the screen at him. "Mr Latimer. You don't know me. I work over at the Omega receiving station at Toronto–"

"How can I help you?"

The man looked nervous, Latimer noticed. "I think you need to know that Omega have been keeping things back from the crew, the colonists–"

"What?" He wondered if some anti-colony nut had managed to get his code.

Caroline was watching him, a worried frown distorting her features.

"The probes," the man went on hurriedly. "Omega said

12

they ceased functioning at around eight years into their journey. Wear and tear, Omega claimed."

"Just who are you?" Latimer said.

"They were lying. The probes didn't degrade naturally, of wear and tear. The Hansen-Spirek coils–"

The connection ceased. The screen filled with snow and static.

Latimer looked across at Caroline and replaced his com-set on the table.

"What do you think he meant?" she asked.

"Beats me. Earth First propaganda?"

Over the course of the previous ten years, the Omega Corporation had sent out four unmanned probes on the approximate course the *Dauntless* was due to take. They had travelled at eighty-five percent of the speed of light, the maximum attainable, and passed the Centauri star system without detecting suitable planets. A couple of months ago telemetry had failed, but Omega scientists had shown a marked reluctance to explain the failings.

His com chimed again.

"Part two," he said grimly.

He snatched up his com. "Yes'?"

Sabine Courvier looked out at him. "Ted, we just intercepted that call."

"What was he on about?" Latimer asked.

"We assume he was a protestor, Ted. I don't know how he managed to get your code."

"What he said about the–" Latimer began.

Courvier smiled. "He's trying to scare you. The latest, desperate tactics of the Earth First mob. They've contacted other crew with stories of systems failures in the Hansen-Spirek coils. All spurious, of course."

"I know that, Sabine."

"Okay, I'll let you get on with your breakfast. See you at

13

twelve." She cut the connection.

Latimer laid the com aside and smiled across at Caroline. "Where were we?" he said.

She laughed. "I was saying how lucky we are," Caroline murmured. She shivered, despite the sunlight. "I really can't imagine remaining on Earth," she went on. "Is it any wonder that jealous people have tried to sabotage the mission?"

They finished breakfast and prepared themselves for the ordeal of leave-taking at noon.

* * *

The reception hall was a huge geodesic on the foreshore, with a view over the ocean and, off to the left, the three shuttles that would whisk the last of the colonists off to the *Dauntless*.

By the time Latimer and Caroline arrived, a little after noon, perhaps a hundred people were standing around the dome in small groups, holding wine glasses and chatting self-consciously.

These were friends and family of the maintenance crew and colonists; Latimer made out Jenny Li, the tiny Korean medic, talking animatedly with her mother, father and awe-stricken younger sister. Friday Emecheta, the Nigerian computer expert, loomed over his wizened mother, while Serena Renfrew, the New Zealander biologist, hugged her weeping sisters and tried to hold back her own tears.

Caroline was fortunate, Latimer thought, in having no close family to say goodbye to today.

He noticed Jenny Li glance over at Emecheta, who pointedly ignored her. Their long-running affair had just ended – or rather, Emecheta had ended it. The atmosphere at maintenance team briefings for the past few weeks had been cryogenic, to say the least.

As team leader, Latimer would have to keep a keen eye on Li and Emecheta during the mission. As if he didn't have enough to occupy his thoughts right now!

Then he saw his father and sister, Sam, with her two boys. They were sitting at a table by the curving wall of the dome, the six year-old twins zooming models of the *Dauntless* over the table-top.

His father, eighty now, stood as Latimer and Caroline approached. There was a second of awkwardness as both men, caught between a lifetime's abjuration of intimacy, and the enormity of the moment, considered whether a hug or a handshake would be in order.

They shook hands. He kissed his sister, hugged the kids.

The conversation was stilted.

"All set?" his father joked. "Bags packed?"

"Now you make sure you look after Ted out there," Sam said to Caroline.

They were saved the embarrassment of further platitudes when Sabine Courvier called for silence and made a short speech along the lines of: *We're all gathered here today to say our farewells to the men and women who are taking humanity to the stars ...*

Latimer shut out the drone, stared into his drink and wished he were out of here and on the shuttle.

Courvier wound down her speech and circulated. A minute later she breezed up to the Latimer's table, introduced herself to the others with false brio and dazzling smiles, and murmured to Latimer: "A quick word, Ted."

He stepped from the table, and Courvier said: "We've apprehended the Earth First saboteur. He got a job at reception over in Dallas, which is how he came by your code. I hope the bastard didn't give you the jitters."

"He began to say something about the Hansen-Spirek coils."

15

"Earth First scare tactics, Ted."

Latimer held her gaze. "It would help if Omega came out with the reason why the probes failed."

Courvier hesitated, then said: "We discovered a bug in the telemetry system here on Earth. We've sorted it out."

"So you'll be able to send us the promised message?" he asked.

When his team awoke for the first maintenance shift, in fifteen hundred years from now, they would be beyond telemetry communication with Earth. But the Omega Corporation would have sent one last message to the *Dauntless* and her crew, thirty years from now, Earth-time. That would be their final link with home. After that, they would be on their own.

Courvier smiled. "Don't worry, we'll bring you up to date on how things are back home." She paused. "So ... everything AOK?"

Latimer said: "I'm fine. So's Caroline. We can't wait to be away."

Courvier nodded, held out a hand and looked into his eyes. "Farewell, Ted. Good luck."

She hugged Caroline, and across the dome the big double doors slid open on to the apron of the port. The assembly within the dome made their slow way into the sunlight.

Latimer felt a tightness within his chest.

A barrier, patrolled by armed Omega Corps guards, demarcated the point beyond which civilians were not allowed.

Latimer turned to his sister, took her in his arms. "Bye, Sam. I love you." He kissed the kids.

Sam grabbed him again, hugged him tight. "You don't know how much I wish I was coming along with you, Ted!"

He felt something like grief fill his chest as he made out

16

the note of envy in her words.

He turned to his father. This time, they did hug.

"So long, Ted. I can't say how proud I am, son." When Latimer pulled away, he saw tears coursing down his father's grey and shrunken cheeks.

"Goodbye," he said, in a little more than a whisper.

Caroline grasped his hand and they turned and walked through the barrier, across the tarmac to the waiting shuttle.

At the top of the ramp, he turned for one last glimpse of his family.

They saw him, and raised their arms in a final, farewell salute.

Thirty minutes later the shuttle took off, banked, and though Latimer peered through the viewscreen at the apron far below, he could not make out the figures of his father or sister.

He sat back in his seat and gripped Caroline's hand, tight.

Two hours later, against the sable velvet of space, he saw the stark grey shape of the *Dauntless*.

He looked the other way, made out the brilliant blue sphere of planet Earth, and the sight of the jewel caused him to take a deep breath. So beautiful …

Farewell, he thought.

The shuttle docked, and they left their seats and entered the access umbilical.

Technicians with com-boards awaited the maintenance crew and colonists.

Latimer turned to Caroline. They would part here, Caroline led to hangar Five and put into cold sleep, while Latimer would make his way to the maintenance unit with Emecheta, Renfrew and Li, where he too would undergo the balm of oblivion.

"See you … soon, Carrie," he said, taking her in his arms.

"Love you," she whispered. "See you, Ted."

17

He led his team along the corridor to the maintenance unit, where the techs waited to put them under.

He sat on the edge of his pod, exchanging smiles with Renfrew and Li.

He had trained for years for this moment, and now it had arrived. He lay in the pod, closed his eyes. He didn't want to look into the jealous eyes of the tech who put him to sleep.

Let's get it over with, he thought.

He felt a dozen sub-dermal capillary needles crawl across his exposed flesh, and then oblivion claimed him.

One

Latimer suffered a succession of lucid dreams before his resuscitation was complete. He was on Earth, an Earth he would never again see, and he was saying goodbye to his family. As is the way with dreams, the images were fragmented, disconnected: one minute he was hugging his frail and ageing father; the next, kissing his sister. Familiar faces morphed into faces less familiar, acquaintances from years earlier, people he had hardly known. Later he wondered if the heightened clarity of the visions had been an effect of the chemicals sluicing through his system, bringing him back to life after so many years in cold sleep.

Then the dreams fell away, and he was hit by a piercing realisation: everyone he'd left on Earth, *everyone*, would be dead by now. His father, his sister and the kids ... dead for centuries. Gone and forgotten. Or almost. He realised that his recollection of them, a tiny focus of firing neurones so many light years from Earth, was the only evidence in the vastness of the universe that they had ever existed.

He felt something cold and hard on his cheek, reached up and touched a frozen tear.

Carrie, he thought. More than anything he wanted to see

his wife again. It would be possible: once they had run though the routine checks, he would have a little time to himself. He would visit hangar Five, where she slept, and watch her dreaming.

He might even have time to do a little jogging. After so long in cold sleep, he needed a workout. He would see what Jenny Li said.

He opened his eyes. He was surprised at how well he felt. He had expected to be beset by aches and pains, headaches. He felt bright and alive, ready for work.

He smiled. This is the furthest anyone has ever been from Earth, he thought. He and his team, and the sleeping colonists, were pushing the envelope of human habitation far, far out into the universe.

He looked at the digital display beside his head, wondering how long he had been under. The figures made no sense to him. The digits flipped over crazily, years apparently passing in seconds.

The cover of his pod was open, revealing a long chamber of white surfaces, banks of consoles and screens. He was aware of movement at the periphery of his vision, and then noise. Voices.

He pushed himself into a sitting position. His unit had prepared a mug of high-energy concentrate. He drank the sweet, milky gloop, then looked across the control unit at Serena Renfrew. She was sitting on the edge of her pod, looking pale and tired.

"How long have we been under?" he asked her.

She shook her head. "My display's down, Ted. According to Emecheta, around a thousand years."

"A thousand?" he said. "But ..." But, if everything had gone to plan, they shouldn't have been awoken for another five hundred years.

Then he heard Emecheta shouting: "Will you lazy set of bastards move yourselves! I said we got an emergency here. You didn't hear the alarms?"

Then Li: "What alarms?"

Latimer wondered if he was dreaming again, a waking nightmare.

Serena Renfrew said: "Heard nothing, Em. What gives?" She sounded sleepy, still drugged.

In the event of an emergency, the team should have been awoken by alarms in each pod. Like Renfrew and Li, Latimer had heard nothing.

He stood, clutching the cover of the pod for support as blood rushed to his head and his vision blurred.

When he felt he could walk without stumbling, he crossed to where the big Nigerian hunched over his com-station. Emecheta's over-sized fingers were playing a frantic arpeggio across the touch-pad.

Latimer was aware of the slight hum, almost a vibration, that conducted itself through the *Dauntless* as it arrowed through space.

Li joined him, diminutive in her red bodysuit. She was hardly taller than the seated figure of Emecheta. She peered at the screen, and the slits of her eyes, set flush in the sallow flesh of her Korean face, narrowed even further.

"Bad news," she said under her breath.

"You don't say?" Emecheta said, without taking his gaze from the scrolling diagnostics.

Latimer said: "What the hell's going on, Em?" The figures made no sense to him, an engineer.

Serena Renfrew left her pod and slumped into a seat before her com-station.

Emecheta pushed himself back on his swivel-chair and nodded. "Okay," he said. "This is what happened. We're a couple of hundred light years from Earth, give or take a few parsecs. We'd attained ninety-five percent of expected velocity. Everything was running smooth. Like a dream, my friends."

"And then ...?" Renfrew said, and dried up.

"And then we ran smack bang into something," Emecheta said. "Something big. Central AI is down. We're running on the auxiliary system integral to this unit, and auxiliary seems to think it was a meteor storm, interstellar debris—"

"What it was hardly matters," Latimer said. "What's the damage?"

"Hard to assess," Emecheta said. "It appears we lost half the ship, maybe two or three of the hangars, a couple of the main drives."

"Jesus," Latimer whispered.

Carrie, he thought.

Jenny Li, beside him, was quietly weeping, trying not to let the others see her. She turned to her com-station and absorbed herself in the screen.

Latimer wiped his brow. He was sweating. His pulse battered through him, abnormally loud. He controlled his breathing. "Okay," he said. "Do you know which hangars are still out there?"

Emecheta fingered the touch-pad, leaning towards the screen and peering at the scrolling columns.

Renfrew reached out and squeezed Latimer's hand. He smiled and nodded at her, the minimal acknowledgement all he was able to give at this moment, lest he break down.

The *Dauntless* carried five hangars, each containing one thousand sleeping human beings. If two or three hangars had been lost in the impact, then the chances were that Carrie's was one of them.

"No way of knowing, Ted," Emecheta said, "with Central AI down."

22

Then Renfrew, instilling Latimer with fresh hope, said: "The screen – surely the main viewscreen's still working?"

With remorseless logic, Emecheta said: "The viewscreen is controlled by Central AI, Serena. Ergo, it's down."

"But we don't know that," Renfrew went on.

Jenny Li pushed her swivel-chair towards a bank of terminals above which, stretching to the curved ceiling, was the long oval of the shielded viewscreen. She tapped commands into a touch-pad. As they looked on, Latimer hardly daring to hope, the shield slowly withdrew from the screen.

It was blank, black.

Li tapped again. "I might be able to patch something through an independent surveillance cam," she said.

Renfrew smiled encouragingly at Latimer.

He tried not to consider the worst case scenario: that hangar Five, and Carrie with it, had been destroyed in the impact.

Li said: "I think I have something here."

As he watched, the screen flickered. He saw brief flashes of the ship's superstructure, diminishing in perspective, set against a backdrop of sable space and distant, twinkling stars.

I'm not going to like this one bit, Latimer thought. Seconds later the image resolved itself, and he found a swivel-chair and slumped into it.

They stared up at the screen in silence.

It was a demoralising scene of destruction, of mangled wreckage, sheared bulkheads and ruptured decks. The control unit in which they sat was a tiny blob on the top of the ship – corresponding to where a whale's blow-hole would be situated – that looked back along the length of the vessel.

The hangars had been positioned on the back of the ship, two each to left and right, and one in the middle. They had been connected by great tubular access routes, through which Latimer and his team could reach each hangar in order to effect any repairs and monitor the health of the sleeping colonists.

Now, it was as if the hangars had suffered a direct hit in some cataclysmic battle.

The impact had destroyed two of the five hangars, those situated on the port side of the *Dauntless*. Where they should have been was now no more than a ragged plain of empty deck. Of the three remaining hangars, number One was intact and still connected to the main body of the ship. Hangar Five, the hangar in which Carrie slept – Latimer saw with a heart-pounding sensation of relief – was still whole, though the access tube leading from the ship to the hangar was pulverised, inaccessible.

Hangar Two had been disconnected from the main body of the ship in the impact: it hung in space a hundred metres above the shattered superstructure, connected to the ship by snaking hank of life-support umbilicals. It floated eerily, canted at an unnatural angle.

So there was hope: Carrie had not perished in the impact. But what was the status of the colonists in hangars Two and Five?

He began to say something, but Li was ahead of him. "I'm trying to find out," she said, hunched over the touch-pad, her fingers flying.

While she worked, Latimer took in the rest of the destruction.

The drive unit to port no longer existed: the sponson on which it had been affixed now terminated roughly fifty meters from the flank of the ship, sheared by the impact. The starboard drive unit still functioned at the end of its sponson, though, the Hanson-Spirek coil burning brightly as it powered the devastated ship onward at just under a third the speed of light.

"We've got to get out there and access hangars Five and Two–" Latimer began.

From behind them, Emecheta said: "I don't see that that's an absolute necessity right now, boss."

Li said: "I'm trying to get a status report on the sleepers. I'm trying to patch something through on auxiliary."

Latimer swivelled his seat and stared at Emecheta.

"Face it," the Nigerian went on, looking around at them. "The chances are that the colonists are okay. Why take a risk going out there?"

Renfrew said: "Have a heart, Em. How would you feel if there was a loved one of yours in hangar Five?"

"But there isn't, Serena. I made sure of that. Remember, I was against couples making the journey right back at committee stage."

Latimer glanced at Jenny Li. She had looked up from her touch-pad and was staring, open-mouthed with shock, at Emecheta.

"So that's it," Latimer said. "You were overruled back then, and you're still sore about it."

"I foresaw a time when having couples along might make for instances of divided interest."

Jenny Li said to Emecheta: "So that's why you dumped me, you heartless bastard!"

The big Nigerian shrugged. "I got out of the relationship because it wasn't working, Jen. As simple as that."

"You cold bastard," Li whispered, shaking her head.

Looking from Latimer to Renfrew, Emecheta went on: "In any situation that might involve the safety of the team, as opposed to that of your wife, Ted, then you might be unable to make the right decision. The right decision for the mission, that is."

25

"You forget the rules laid down at committee stage, Em," Latimer said, reasonably. "My decision is not final. We work on democratic principles."

"But you have the right of veto, Ted. And what about influence? Do you think Jen and Serena would go against anything our elected leader might command?"

Li turned back to her console in disgust. Renfrew said: "Give us a little credit, Em. We're quite capable of thinking for ourselves."

Latimer stepped in before the situation could escalate. "Enough, okay? This is hardly the time for in-fighting. We have a major incident on our hands here. As I see it, we need to assess the status of the sleepers in the damaged hangars. That'd be my decision even if Carrie wasn't out there–"

Jenny Li looked up from her com-station. "I'm getting something."

Latimer leaned over her shoulder and read the text scrolling down the screen. It was a list of maintenance diagnostics from hangars Two and Five. They were functioning at well within the safety limit of ninety-nine percent.

Emecheta said: "So ... you still think it necessary to go out there, boss?"

Ignoring the Nigerian, Latimer turned to Li. "What do you think?"

She said: "The sleepers are doing fine, Ted." She indicated the diagnostics. "In Five, there's damage to the access tubes, but nothing more."

"What about Two?" Latimer asked, staring out to where the disconnected hangar floated against a backdrop of stars.

"Same again. It might look bad, but it's still connected to the power supply. The sleepers are AOK."

"Is there anything we could do to bring Two down to the

26

deck, secure it there?" he asked, looking at Emecheta.

The Nigerian shook his head. "It'd be too big a job. I say we leave it as is. Remember, there's no friction out there. It isn't in any danger. The power supply's working – that's the main thing."

Latimer nodded and stared through the screen, at the wreckage of the starship. On the deck, between torn shards of metal, he made out the tiny, scuttling forms of a hundred or more robot drones, trilobite-analogues and bigger, legged roboids, mindlessly obeying the dictates of their programming. These robots – perhaps a thousand units of various sizes and designs – had worked for ten centuries at routine tasks, minor maintenance and repair. They were self-servicing, taking parts from the automated manufactory in the bowels of the ship to replace those bits of themselves worn out or damaged down the years. They were overseen by Central AI and its various subsidiary routines.

As Latimer watched them, he wondered at how their functioning had been affected by the damage to Central AI. That was Emecheta's specialism.

"If Central's down, how come the roboids and drones are still functioning?"

Emecheta nodded at his console. "I thought of that. While you were still sleeping, I patched the few lone drones into the auxiliary system and got them working again."

Latimer nodded. "Well done. We'll be relying on the drones over the next few thousand years. We can't afford any dysfunction at this stage of the mission."

Li looked up from her com-station, her expression shocked.

"What is it?" Latimer asked.

She was shaking her head. "I've just checked the ship's log. With everything going on when we awoke, it never occurred to me."

27

"Nor me," Latimer admitted. "Go on."

"Well," Li said, "according to the log, we've been in flight for a little over one thousand and eighty years. In that time, we've covered not quite two hundred light years."

Latimer nodded. The figures were an abstraction he had no real hope of understanding. They had travelled farther than any human before them – they were pushing the limits of exploration in a way that, twenty-five years earlier, before the development of the Hanson-Spirek coil, no-one would have thought possible.

Such a fragile cargo of life in the infinite depths of space.

Guessing where this was leading, Latimer said: "Two hundred light years – so, how many planetary systems did we investigate?"

Li glanced at Renfrew, then said: "Twenty."

"Twenty?" he echoed. What had Omega forecast? That the chances were they would discover a habitable planet – or at least a planet that might prove adaptable – within ten attempts?

"And not one of them matched Omega's wide criteria for a liveable planet," Li went on. "Not one. Nothing." She gestured to the screen. "It's all there, planet after barren, hostile planet. Twenty worlds matched the criteria insofar as distance from primary, but all failed when it came to biosphere make-up and atmosphere content. There wasn't even one world back there we could terraform with any hope of success."

"Jesus Christ," Latimer said. The parameters that the Omega Corporation had set for terraforming had been pretty elastic. With the cold sleep facility, the colonists could wait out something in the order of twenty thousand years, while a planet was remade, before systems degradation kicked in.

Into the following silence, Emecheta said: "So where does that leave us?"

28

"I've made a few calculations," Li said, "extrapolating from the data gathered so far. I don't know ... I can't be sure ... I'd really like Central to back me up on this, but Central's down, so..."

"Jenny," Latimer said, exasperated.

"Well, I calculated that going by the data gathered so far, then it might be another thirty thousand years before we find a suitable Earth-like, or even terraformable, planet."

In the sudden silence, Latimer could hear the ticking of his heart, the slight movement of Renfrew's chair as she rocked back and forth, and Emecheta's heavy breathing.

He nodded. "Okay, thanks for that, Jenny." He sat down and looked around at his team. "Does anyone have any comments?"

Emecheta merely stared down at his big hands. Renfrew just shook her head, appalled. Li could not meet his gaze.

"Jenny?" he asked.

"Well, I just wondered ... I thought maybe we might consider the possibility of turning back."

The words seemed to freeze the very air of the chamber.

After perhaps five seconds, Emecheta laughed. "Turn back to what, girl? Get real. Earth's probably blown itself to hell and back!"

Latimer said: "We can't turn back, even if we knew Earth was AOK." He paused, gathering his thoughts. "So you think we won't come across a habitable planet for thirty thousand years, based on data gathered so far. But that doesn't rule out the chance that we might – just might – come across something within the next twenty thousand years before degradation sets in. We've got to keep on."

Li looked forlorn. "But how long do we go on before we decide that enough's enough? What if we haven't come across a suitable planet in that time? The cold sleep system will be so degraded it'll be useless, with no hope of repair. What then?"

"We'll have found a suitable planet by that time, Jenny. You studied Omega's predictions. We all agreed with them back then."

"Predictions," the Korean countered. "What we're faced with now are hard facts. Evidence."

Latimer took a deep breath. "So okay, we turn back. We return to Earth – if it's still there – in what? Far longer than the thousand years it took us to get this far, now that we're travelling on one drive. Can you imagine that?" He looked around at his team. "Let's assume, for the sake of argument, that Earth's survived. We won't be going back to the place we knew. Society, human beings, will have changed out of all recognition. So much will have happened in the time we've been away – we'll have no hope of understanding or fitting in. We'll be freaks."

He stopped, aware of the eyes on him.

"And remember, we'd be consigning not only the four of us to a world we no longer recognised or belonged to," – he indicated the viewscreen, the hangars containing the three thousand sleepers – "we'd be playing with the destiny of everyone else, too. Think about that."

In the long, silent seconds that ensued, they thought about it.

We can't vote to go back, he thought. It would be more than just defeat, it would be the end of a dream.

"So … what do you think? Who's for pressing on?"

Help came from an unexpected source. Emecheta raised a big hand. "I'm with the boss. I say we keep on. We can't turn back now. We signed up to do a job, and like Ted says, even if Earth survived, what kind of Earth would we be returning to? We'd be like Neanderthals among Homo Sapiens."

30

Latimer looked across at Emecheta and nodded his thanks. He turned to Renfrew. "You?"

He could see the uncertainty in her eyes. Finally she gave in and nodded. "As I see it, we're caught between two evils," Renfrew said. "I don't like the picture Jenny paints – I don't like the idea of just going on and on and on without hope – but what would we be going back to, if anything? So, yes, let's keep on."

"I think you know how I feel on the issue," Latimer said. "So we press on. Okay, Jenny?"

She gave her head a minimal nod. "It was only a suggestion, Ted. I ... I'd like to go back. I'm sure Earth has pulled through. But I guess I'm out-voted on this one."

She turned her seat and regarded the screen.

Renfrew said: "Hey ... Did you check for incoming, Jenny? What about that message from Earth?"

Even before Jenny Li replied, Latimer knew the answer.

The Korean shook her head. "If Earth did broadcast, and we did pick it up, it was lost with the damage to Central."

The news was yet another disappointment. How wonderful it would have been to have heard from the Omega Corporation, told that all was bright and rosy on a rejuvenated planet Earth. But, thinking about it, perhaps it was just as well the message had been lost. If the news from Earth had been unremittingly bleak ...

For the next hour they prepared themselves for another stretch of cold sleep. Emecheta set the program to wake them after a thousand years, and they returned to their pods. Li and Renfrew lay down and pulled the covers shut over themselves, and in seconds the alpha-numerics were sequencing along the flanks of their pods, denoting successful immersion.

Latimer was about to settle into his own pod when he looked across the unit at Emecheta. "Hey, I appreciate your

31

help back there. We're doing the right thing."

"Sure, boss," Emecheta said. And with that, he lay down and drew the cover over himself.

Latimer smiled to himself and stretched out in his pod. He felt the tickle of a dozen hypodermic capillaries worming under his skin, and seconds later he was sinking as if under the most sublime anaesthetic.

His last waking thought was that Carrie was alive and well, and he entered cold sleep with a vision of her beauty playing in his mind's eye.

Two

It seemed to Latimer that he came awake almost immediately and rose slowly through a sea of dreams. He saw a twisted, phantasmagoric image of the starship, wrecked beyond salvation, and a thousand floating bodies.

The cover above him lifted suddenly. It was Renfrew, staring down at him.

"We got a problem, Ted."

"No suitable colony planets?" he said, half awake.

"No – but that's not the problem."

He sat up and swung himself from the pod, but too fast. His vision swam as he stood. He felt dizzy, nauseous. Renfrew passed him a beaker of high-energy concentrate. He gagged half of it down, then pushed himself over to where Emecheta and Li were hunched over their com-stations.

"What's happening?"

They were too intent on the screens to explain. He turned to Renfrew. "How long have we been out?"

"A thousand years, like we programmed."

"So we weren't pulled out by the emergency alarm?"

She shook her head. "As soon as I woke, I checked things at my com-station. Central's as dead as before – and

33

something's happened to the auxiliary back-up. It's down. We've got no link to the hangars."

Emecheta turned to him. "I don't understand this, Ted. Everything was AOK when we went under. This shouldn't have happened."

Li looked up from her station. "No link to the log, either, Ted. We're completely cut off."

"Okay, so what about the ship? Are we still maintaining speed and course?"

Emecheta shrugged. "No way of knowing."

"Visually?" Latimer suggested. "Can we open the viewscreen?"

Li shook her head. "I tried. Nothing."

Latimer paced to the end of the unit and back. The *Dauntless* was still moving. The constant, thrumming vibration conducted itself through the superstructure of the starship and entered his bones, just as it had done a thousand years earlier.

"Perhaps it's a link problem," Renfrew said. "Central's still functioning, but we've been cut off."

Emecheta considered that. "No way. What about the override circuit? We should be able to get through on some link if Central was still up and running."

Latimer was aware that all eyes were on him. "Our first priority is the sleepers," he said. "First we make sure the systems in the hangars are working. Then we drop to the core and see if we can work out what gives with Central."

The others nodded.

"Em and Serena, check hangar One. Jenny, we'll see if we can get through to hangar Five."

They took the dropshaft to the main lateral corridor, a featureless grey tunnel with all the aesthetics of a storm-drain. They stepped from the plate and crossed to the entry hatch.

34

Latimer tapped the access code into the control unit and stood back.

Nothing happened.

Renfrew glanced at him. "You hit the right code?" she asked.

He tapped it again. "Five – zero – two – five. Open sesame."

The hatch remained shut.

Emecheta pushed past him. "Let me try." He tapped the code and waited, with no result. "Christ!" He removed the cover of the control unit, pulled tools from his belt-pack, and began tinkering. "Overriding the command signal," he said. "This should do the trick."

"In your dreams," Renfrew commented, when the hatch remained closed.

"If we can't get to the hangars …" Li began, voicing what Latimer was thinking.

"And the AI systems are down," he finished.

Carrie … he thought. From one nightmare scenario to another.

"Okay," he said. "Serena, go get the cutting tools from stores."

"I'll help you," Li said.

Emecheta looked at him. "So," he said, when the women had taken the upshaft. "What the hell gives?"

"Beats me. Omega never prepared us for this kind of emergency." He paused, then said: "What about the roboids? They service the sleepers, right? You slaved them to auxiliary, and auxiliary is down."

Emecheta nodded. "Right."

A feeling very much like despair opened up inside Latimer. The sleep pods could function for a thousand years or so, just so long as nothing went wrong. In the event of

35

some mechanical dysfunction, in theory there were always drones on hand to fix things.

But with Central and auxiliary down, and the drones leaderless ...

"Christ knows how many sleepers we might have lost, boss," Emecheta murmured.

Renfrew and Li returned, hauling a big cutter and a tool box.

Li primed the laser-cutter, the bulky device incongruous when wielded by an operator as diminutive as the Korean. She stood with it lodged on her hip and applied the working end of the cutter to the hatch.

It burned, sending up a plume of acrid smoke.

She worked with painstaking care, slicing a vertical line through the metal. When she reached the floor, Emecheta took over. He cut a line at right-angles to the vertical slice, then downwards to create a small door-shape.

Five minutes later he killed the cutter, placed it on the floor and kicked at the crude door-shape with his right boot. The section of metal fell away and landed on the corridor beyond with a loud, ringing clang.

He stood back, grinning. "After you," he said, indicating the aperture.

Latimer ducked and made to ease himself through.

The laser vector almost decapitated him. He felt the heat of it as it passed over his shoulder, was aware of an instant of blinding white light, then felt hands on his legs, hauling him back. A second vector lanced through the opening, missing him by centimetres.

He lay on the floor next to Emecheta, who had evidently saved his life. Renfrew was backed up against the bulkhead, knuckles to her mouth, staring at him.

Li was already unfastening her medi-kit and fishing out

36

some kind of salve. She applied it to his neck, even before Latimer realised he'd been burned.

Then she hit him with a hypo-ject. "Pain-killer," she explained. "Christ, you were lucky, Ted."

He stood and moved away from the opening in the hatch, staring at the laser burn on the far wall. "What the hell was that?" he said.

"How about this?" Em said. "A rogue drone. One of those factory critters. One of Central's slaves has gone berserk."

Latimer stared at him. "They can do that?"

The Nigerian shrugged. "Any other suggestions?"

Li said: "What about the sleepers, Ted?" in a small, frightened voice.

Latimer's belly contracted, and he nearly vomited the concentrate he'd forced down on awakening.

Carrie ...

"We should arm ourselves," he said. "There's no telling if it'll try to come through."

Emecheta nodded and picked up the cutter from the floor. He moved to the hatch and positioned himself next to the aperture, the cutter poised to slice anything that might venture through.

"Jenny," Latimer said, "break out four lasers from stores. Serena, go with her. Bring back one of those remote surveillance cams and a monitor, okay?"

The two women ran to the upshaft and disappeared.

"Another thing they never trained us to cope with," Emecheta grinned.

"I'm an engineer, Em, not a damned soldier. I volunteered for the mission to build a new world out there, not fight rogue drones."

"Know why I volunteered?"

Latimer smiled. "To drive me nuts?"

37

"Apart from that," Emecheta said. He glanced at the hatch, then back to Latimer. "The challenge. Adventure. I thought, who knows what we'll find out there? One thing I was sure about, though. We could beat it. Ingenuity, logic. We can beat anything if we just think it through, okay?"

"Hope you're right, Em," Latimer said, and thought again of Carrie.

The dropshaft purred, lowering the women back down. They carried two laser pistols apiece. Li had the surveillance cam and monitor in a backpack.

The cam was a tiny flyer, about the size of a dragonfly. Latimer set the monitor on the deck well away from the hatch and readied the cam. It lifted, bobbed. He experimented with the controls, finally managed to patch a picture through to the monitor. The image was grainy, showing an unstable image of the corridor as the cam rose and fell.

Emecheta lay aside the cutter and joined the others behind the monitor. He took up a pistol, directing it at the hatch, while Latimer manoeuvred the dragonfly cam. It hovered towards the hatch and disappeared through the cut-away section.

All eyes were on the monitor.

The corridor was in darkness until the passing of the cam tripped a sequence of dim wall lights. Even then, the image was indistinct. Latimer made out the ribbed walls and grey floor of the corridor, broken by frequent static, some dysfunction of the telemetry phasing the image from colour to granular black and white.

Latimer estimated that the cam had travelled about five metres when he made out a squat, four-legged shape in the centre of the screen.

Li pointed. "A manufactory drone," she said. "What the hell's that doing up here?"

38

Then Latimer made out a host of other drones and roboids behind it, a veritable regiment. He peered, squinting.

The drone was advancing. As he watched, it extended something from the bulk of its body and fired.

He heard a small explosion in the corridor beyond, and the image on the monitor went blank.

Then he heard a quick skittering sound coming from beyond the hatch.

The drone appeared in the cut-away section of the hatch and let go with a volley of laser fire. Latimer returned fire, along with Emecheta, hitting the drone with little apparent effect. A stray vector struck Emecheta and he cried out in pain.

Li ran towards the dropshaft and yelled at the others to join her. While Renfrew laid down a constant hail of laser fire, Latimer hauled Emecheta on to the up-plate. Renfrew came last, still firing, and the second she was on the plate, Latimer stabbed the controls and they rose towards the command unit and safety.

Three

"You'll live," Li said. She applied a seal of synthi-flesh to the wound on Emecheta's upper arm, then administered a hypoject analgesic.

Latimer locked the hatch to the dropshaft. Emecheta looked across at him. "You think that'll hold?"

"They can't open it from the underside," Latimer said.

"What about with cutting tools?"

Latimer was silent for a second, then said: "I'd rather not think about that."

Li was staring at them, wide-eyed. "You don't think they …?"

Emecheta flexed his injured arm. "Who the hell knows what to think? Who'd think the drones'd arm themselves and attack us in the first place? Some bad shit's gone down back there."

Into the following silence, Renfrew said quietly: "Did anyone else see it?"

Latimer looked across the unit at her. She had been silent since reaching the safety of the unit, sitting by herself on a swivel-chair and nursing her pistol.

"What?" he asked.

"On the monitor, behind the drone and the other roboids. I thought I saw ..." She fell silent, shaking her head.

Emecheta said: "What the fuck, Serena, do you think you saw?"

Renfrew looked up at the staring faces. "You mean, none of you saw it?"

"For chrissake," Latimer said.

"I could swear I saw a figure, a human figure. It was standing at the end of the corridor, in the shadows."

Latimer felt an icy shiver pass down his spine.

"Impossible!" he said. "Listen, the pods were programmed to wake the sleepers at journey's end. There's no way they could've–"

"Hey, boss," Emecheta said, quietly. "You forget who's in charge down there, now."

Li said: "But why would they wake up a sleeper?"

"Listen," Latimer said. "Serena said she *thought* she saw a figure. The lighting down there wasn't so good, was it? So she was mistaken."

Emecheta moved towards the dropshaft.

"Where the hell do you think you're going?" Latimer said.

"There's only one way to settle this. I'll get the monitor. It'll have recorded everything the cam relayed."

"You want another laser burn, this time in your chest?"

Emecheta ignored him. He took Li's laser and, a pistol in each hand, unlocked the dropshaft hatch and stepped onto the plate.

"Emecheta!" Latimer said. He almost lifted his pistol, then, and threatened the Nigerian. Something stopped him, the realisation that nothing would prevent Emecheta from retrieving the monitor.

"Don't worry, boss, I'll take care."

He dropped.

41

Latimer ran to the aperture in the floor and stared down. Emecheta was crouching on the drop-plate, hand on the controls, inching his way down. There was no sign of the rogue drone down there, or any of its cohorts – which didn't mean a thing. If one of them were in hiding beyond the hole in the hatch, just waiting for a human to show himself ...

The drop-plate reached the deck. The monitor lay where Latimer had left it, about a metre from the shaft. All Emecheta had to do was reach out and grab it.

He reached, got hold of the monitor and pulled it towards him – and then the firing began. A tracery of white light volleyed from the cut-away section of the hatch, filling the corridor with a blinding, actinic glare. Emecheta yelled out, whether in crazed delight at battle joined, or in pain, Latimer had no idea. The Nigerian returned fire and stabbed the up-plate command, and Latimer watched him rise towards the control unit as white light rained all around him.

He hauled Emecheta from the plate and locked the hatch, silencing the noise of the lasers. "You okay?"

"Told you I'd take care," he laughed, laying the monitor on a workbench. "Now let's see if you were seeing things, Serena."

They gathered around the monitor while Emecheta accessed the file and replayed the images, from the time the cam entered the far corridor to the moment of its destruction.

"There!" Renfrew said, pointing.

Emecheta froze the image.

Behind the laser-wielding drone, Latimer made out the indistinct figure of a human being. There was no doubt about it. The figure stood in the opening to hangar one, seemingly watching the advance of the drone.

"What in Christ's name ..." Emecheta whispered.

He ran the image at real-time. The figure stepped back into the hangar, and a second later the monitor went blank as the cam

42

was destroyed.

"Get the figure again," Latimer said. "Magnify it."

Emecheta did so, zoomed in on the shadowy figure. The image became even grainier, but now they could see that the figure was that of a man.

Emecheta froze the image and looked up. "So what gives?"

"Maybe they're holding the sleepers hostage in there," Li suggested.

"We're talking about slave drones!" Renfrew objected. "Machines about as dumb as your average holo-player."

"It was a drone nearly did for us down there," Emecheta said. "It came after us, fired with intent."

"Maybe ..." Li said in a small voice, "maybe it'd been reprogrammed?"

"By whom?" Emecheta laughed.

She shrugged. "By Central. I don't know, maybe the meteor impact sent Central crazy. Knocked out its Omega programming. It's self-repairing, isn't it? Don't Central AIs have the ability to learn, upgrade? Maybe it repaired itself ... But it's decided not to tell us."

"Look," Latimer cut in, "I don't have a clue what's going on down there. The simple fact is that the sleepers are in danger, agreed?"

Everyone nodded.

He waited a beat, then said: "So what do we do?"

Li looked away. Renfrew pulled a face, considering.

Only Emecheta looked him in the eye. He said: "We get into the hangars, check out what's happening." He paused. "Only trouble is, the drones seem to have the lateral corridor pretty well covered, as far as I see it."

"So we don't go in through the front door," Latimer said. "We get into our EVA suits, leave this unit through the

43

emergency hatch and access the nearest hangar – hangar One – through its own emergency exit."

"And just hope that they don't have drones covering the exit," Emecheta said.

Latimer looked around at his team. "I think two of us should go, two stay behind. I'm going. Any other volunteers?"

Emecheta nodded. "Count me in."

Four

They suited up, cycled themselves through the emergency air-lock, and attached the safety cables. They were high above the body of the ship, looking down on the wrecked superstructure stretching aft.

Hangar One was perhaps a hundred metres below where they stood on the lip of the air-lock. Their destination, the emergency exit, was situated on the near flank, highlighted by a crimson circle like a bull's eye.

Hangar Five, where Carrie lay in innocent oblivion, was positioned beyond hangar One, its access tube mashed in the impact a thousand years earlier. High above the tortured decking, hangar Two hung on a length of umbilical leads, moving lazily like submarine vegetation in a slight current.

Latimer nodded to Emecheta and stepped from the lock. He felt the kick of his powerpack as it cut in and he steered himself through the vacuum towards the hangar.

A minute later he came down gently amid the scattered debris of radio antennae and microwave relays. They picked their way slowly through an obstacle course of twisted metal, Latimer aware that a cut from one of the many razor-sharp shards could depressurise his suit and kill him in seconds.

At one point he stopped and stared around him at the destruction. He examined the damage, the way the metal of the deck had been sheared and excoriated. Grotesque spars and girders arched above them, like the skeletal structure of a bombed-out Gothic cathedral.

He pointed. "What do you make of it, Em?"

"The damage?" Emecheta's voice sounded tinny over the radio link.

"Does it look like meteor or cometary damage to you?"

Emecheta, bulky in his padded black and yellow EVA suit, bobbed in position as he took in the destruction. "Hard to say. Never seen a cometary impact before."

Latimer gave voice to his fears. "Looks to me, Em, more like an explosion. The metal appears melted, cut through in some places–"

The Nigerian turned his great helmet and stared at Latimer. "Were you contacted that last day by some Earth First crazy?"

Latimer nodded. "He said Omega were holding back some information. The probes hadn't failed naturally. He said something about the drives–"

Emecheta cut in: "So perhaps the Hansen-Spirek coil blew … That'd explain the destruction."

Latimer's stomach turned sickeningly with the thought that, if they were right, and the Omega Corporation had known all along about the instability of the drives …

It was too much to take on board, right now.

Emecheta gestured. "We're wasting time."

They covered the last few metres to hangar One and paused. The red-painted exit faced Latimer, an arm's length away. Emecheta, perhaps sensing Latimer's hesitation, hopped past him. "Let's do it."

The Nigerian drew his laser and approached the emergency exit.

46

Latimer followed. It should have been so much easier than this, he thought. What had the Omega officials said? Plain sailing … The phrase took on a cynical meaning, if his suspicions proved correct. He tried to push the thought to the back of his mind.

They attached their safety cables to the lugs on either side of the hatch, and Emecheta punched the code. The hatch slid open. They pulled themselves into the air-lock, and the ship's gravity took hold. Latimer faced the inner door. He realised he was sweating, the liquid dribbling down his face, tickling him. He had no way of scratching his cheek.

He told himself to ignore it, concentrate on the task ahead. This is a reconnaissance mission, Emecheta had said while suiting up. We assess the situation and then get out.

The inner door slid open and they stepped, cautiously, into a darkened cavern.

On his suit relay, he heard Emecheta: "Okay, we're on the gallery overlooking the aisles. Let's head for the rail and take a look."

He led the way, Latimer following. His eyes adjusted to the darkness, which was alleviated only by the dim jade halation of a thousand alpha-numeric displays on the pods down below, and an erratic flashing white light somewhere on the far side of the hangar.

Latimer joined Emecheta by the rail and looked down.

"Christ on crutches," Emecheta said. "Will you take a look at that."

The first fact that Latimer took in was that the majority of the pods were open, their covers thrown back and the berths no longer occupied.

Then he saw the colonists.

He thought he was about to vomit in his suit, but managed to gag down a mouthful of vile-tasting bile.

47

There were about fifty colonists lying at the far end of the hangar, the area given over to lockers and showers. It was hard to tell if all of them were dead, but certainly no human being could have survived what had been done to the majority of the sleepers down there.

He saw halved bodies, torsos with limbs and heads removed. Sectioned arms and legs littered the deck, the scene all the more ghastly for being so dimly lit. Like something from the hellish paintings of Hieronymus Bosch.

He felt a touch on his upper arm, and started. "Look," Emecheta said, pointing.

Latimer followed the direction of the Nigerian's gloved hand and made out something moving on the far side of the hangar.

Whatever it was had passed behind a pod, but a second later came back into full view – and Latimer wished that it had remained hidden. There are some things we wish we had never seen, he thought. This was one of them. He would remember this image, he knew, to his dying day.

Later, back in the command unit, he tried to describe what he had seen to Renfrew and Li, but his powers of description failed him.

It had once been human – or at least a part of it had. He thought he could detect where the human vestiges ended and the machine parts began, but it was not easy. It resembled a crab, with the carapace of a menial manufactory drone, and the multiple arms and legs of a human being. They scuttled along in a sequence all the more grotesque for being mistimed, some limbs tripping others and entangling themselves.

The thing stumbled towards the hatch and disappeared into the corridor.

Then Latimer saw colonists not quite so fatally ravaged.

These walked upright, seemingly with intent. They had had machine parts grafted onto their heads and backs, hanks of cabling trailing from their skulls like ghastly dreadlocks, and Latimer only hoped that the consciousness governing their movements was machine – that the humans had died quick deaths long ago.

Is this a localised phenomenon, he found himself thinking, restricted to this hangar, or is the same carnage going on in the other two?

Before he could follow up this thought, Emecheta gripped his arm and yelled: "Down!"

Latimer ducked. The laser vector missed by a good metre, and then he saw why. The creature wielding the rifle was a trilobite 'droid with a single human arm affixed to its shell, and it gripped the rifle clumsily.

It fired again, and then Latimer was running along the gallery after Emecheta. Behind the trilobite, other machine-human amalgams gave chase. Latimer turned. Access to the emergency exit was blocked by the advancing monsters.

"Where to?" Latimer yelled.

The reply rang in his helmet: "Down the steps, across the hangar and into the corridor. Keeping running and firing …"

They came to a steep flight of metal steps and clattered down, their movement impeded by their bulky EVA suits.

They had the element of surprise on their side. Latimer ran and fired indiscriminately, sending machine-human creatures skittering away across the blood-soaked deck. Once he lost his footing on a thick slick of offal, righted himself and ran on, firing.

He wanted to ask Emecheta where the hell he was leading him, but he could not articulate the words through fear. They were running further into danger, and as far as he could see there was no way out.

49

Occasional laser fire came their way, but ill-directed. He followed Emecheta across the hangar, past the area where the fifty bodies lay cannibalised, like a cross between an abattoir and a battlefield.

Emecheta came to the exit hatch and paused. He leaned around the opening, looking up and down the corridor, then turned to Latimer. "This is where the first drone zapped the cam," he said.

Then Latimer knew what Emecheta had in mind. They were next to the corridor where they had sliced an opening through the hatch. If they could make it through the hatch and to the upshaft, they might yet get away.

Emecheta said: "Okay. Follow me. Fire at anything that moves. Turn left and run. Now!"

He vanished around the corner. Latimer gave chase, yelling and firing at a figure that scuttled across the corridor towards him. His shot hit something soft and bloody, and later he wondered if he had sliced in two a living, sentient human being.

Ahead, he made out the Nigerian's lumbering figure and, beyond, the hatch with the neat rectangular section cut into its lower half. Then he saw the laser-wielding drone and opened fire. He hit it, but with little effect. This was an armour-plated industrial 'bot, designed to last many thousand years' wear and tear. A random laser strike was hardly going to penetrate its steel carapace and do it lasting damage.

It turned its laser on the approaching figures and opened fire. Emecheta dodged the vector, but Latimer was not fast enough. He felt the heat of the laser sear through the padding of his EVA suit, scorching his thigh on the way through. To his amazement he was still running.

Then Emecheta reached the drone and kicked out, and where laser fire had failed, the brute efficacy of a boot worked wonders. The rifle flipped from the drone's grip and hit the far bulkhead. Latimer sprinted towards the opening in the hatch, Emecheta after him.

He ducked through, cursed as the raw steel edge snagged at his suit. He tore himself free and stood. When he looked behind him, Emecheta was squirming though the gap. He went back and hauled the Nigerian out by the arms, and together they stumbled towards the upchute.

Laser fire lanced through the aperture after them. They made the chute, stabbed the controls, and turned in time to see the mutilated upper-half of what had once been a woman struggle through the gap.

They rose towards the circular hatch high above them, and Latimer realised that he had locked it what seemed like hours ago now. He snapped the clasp on his helmet and called out for someone to open the hatch. The plate halted and he reached up with his pistol and slammed it into the underside of the hatch, creating a sound like all the drums in the universe.

Below, he made out the figure of the once-human as it paused, lifted its laser rifle and took aim. Beside him, Emecheta held his pistol at arm's length.

"May God take pity on me," he whispered, and fired.

The shot hit the woman between the eyes, and above them the hatch sprang open to reveal the frightened face of Jenny Li.

Five

"Cyborgs," Emecheta said, peeling away his EVA suit and casting it across the room.

Latimer sat against the wall, holding a cold salve to his blistered thigh. He breathed hard and listened to Emecheta. Li passed him a beaker of iced water and he drank gratefully.

"You wouldn't believe what it's like down there!" the Nigerian was saying. "I hope that's the closest I ever come to hell, my friends."

Renfrew looked across at Latimer, as if for an explanation. "Ted, what happened?"

Latimer shook his head. He decided to keep quiet about the suspected cause of the destruction: they had enough to worry about, right now. "Don't know whether it happened at the time of the impact, or as a direct result of it later. Central's lost sight of its prime directive – to serve us."

"But I thought Central was down?" Li said.

Latimer shrugged. "My guess is that its programming was knocked out a thousand years ago, and since then it's reprogrammed itself. Evolved."

Renfrew said: "It found so many units of organic matter in the hangars and used them. Experimented with them."

The silence stretched, and then Li asked the question that Latimer had been loathe to ask himself: "The thing is … are we safe? I mean, will the cyborgs come after us?"

Emecheta said: "So far they've only attacked us when we invaded their territory. They've shown no desire to come after us. Maybe we're okay for the time being."

"For the time being?" Li asked, staring at him. "You mean, until they evolve and need to expand, take over all the ship?"

Latimer cut in: "We don't know they'll do that. I think we're okay for now."

"What about the other sleepers?" Renfrew asked. "Those in hangars Two and Five? The success of the mission depends on their survival."

Latimer looked up. "You don't think I hadn't thought of that?" he asked, despair opening up inside him like physical pain.

Renfrew shrugged. "So what do we do?"

"Maybe the sleepers in Two are okay," Emecheta said. "They might've been saved by the fact that the hangar was blown off the deck. I reckon the drones and roboids have no way of getting to it."

"And hangar Five?" Latimer said.

He thought of Carrie, and what he'd seen in hangar One, and despaired.

Emecheta shrugged. "We could get in via the emergency hatch and hope to Christ the AIs haven't got there before us."

"Maybe they haven't," Latimer said, with appalling optimism. "Maybe they haven't been able to get in through the mangled access tubes …"

Emecheta nodded. "If it is all clear, we wake the sleepers and arm them. Then we stand a fighting chance of defeating the … the cyborgs." He shook his head. "Hell, we might even make a success of the mission yet."

Latimer nodded. "I'll go alone. There's no need anyone else risking themselves."

Emecheta said: "Don't you think you ought to take some time out?"

"With Carrie in there?" Latimer snapped.

Emecheta raised both hands, as if to defend himself.

Li said: "I'll come with you. It's my turn. I haven't been out there yet."

"I said I'll go alone, okay?"

Li shrugged, looked away.

"Don't take any risks," Renfrew said. "If the AIs have got in there, no heroics, okay? Just get back here, and we'll assess the situation."

He ate a tasteless meal from stores, high energy concentrates to rebuild his strength. Talk was desultory at the table. No-one made any further mention of the worst case scenario: that the AIs had already infiltrated hangar Five. No one looked ahead and planned what they should do in that eventuality.

If that's what I find, Latimer thought as he broke out a new EVA suit, then I don't really care what happens.

Six

He left the air-lock and propelled himself through the vacuum, out over the girdered surface of hangar One, trying to shut his mind from the horrors taking place down there.

He was aware of the sound of his heavy breathing. He could see along the length of the ship, the shattered ruins of the superstructure, hangar Five in the distance and Two floating eerily high above.

He hit the deck and paused. Hangar Five stood ten metres to his right, the tube that should have given access to the main body of the ship a flattened mess of metal and circuitry.

Perhaps the AIs haven't got in there yet, he tried to reassure himself again. Perhaps the sleepers are still alive. I'll wake Carrie and explain the situation, then rouse the others. We'll arm ourselves, suit up and repel the cyborgs.

He wished he had radio contact with the others, voices to keep him company. But Emecheta, wisely, had vetoed the idea: the AIs might be monitoring radio communications, he'd warned; better not take the risk.

Latimer felt very lonely, very vulnerable, as he bounced across the deck towards the hangar.

He approached the bull's eye markings of the emergency

exit and tapped in the code. The hatch slid open and he stepped inside. He cycled himself through, raising his pistol in readiness as the inner door slid open.

He was met by darkness, silence.

He took a step forward, cautiously, and peered along the length of the gallery. There was no sign of any AIs. All was in shadow. Ahead, over the main well of the hangar, the dim glow of the pods' running lights was the only illumination.

Hardly daring to hope, he hurried from the emergency exit towards the rail and peered over into the dimness.

All was still, quiet.

He scanned the pods. The covers were lowered, denoting that their occupants were still inside, sleeping soundly. Then, before he allowed elation to grip him, he saw other pods in the rows beyond, whose covers had been opened, and his stomach turned sickeningly.

He scanned the deck, but there was no sign of the wholesale carnage that had taken place in hangar One.

Okay, he thought: perhaps the AIs haven't got here yet. Perhaps the covers are up for other reasons. There might have been fatalities along the way – the possibility had not been ruled out by the Omega medics. Or perhaps the slave drones here had detected malfunctions in certain tanks, and roused the occupants while their pods were repaired.

Even as he considered these scenarios, he knew he was deluding himself.

He hurried along the length of the gallery until he reached the flight of metal stairs. He descended step by step, making as little noise as was possible in the clumsy suit, readying his pistol and turning his head constantly to take in the entirety of the hangar.

He reached the first row and lifted the cover of the closest pod, and his heart sank. It was empty. He moved along to the next pod, paused, and then eased up the cover. This one, too, had been vacated.

After that he hurried to aisle B, then counted along the row until he came to pod 46. He paused, his heart hammering, and only after long seconds did he lift the cover. He knew what he would find, but even so, the sight of the empty berth filled him with despair.

He moved across the hangar, checking a few pods on every row. Every one was the same. They were empty. The sleepers had been removed.

The question was: where were they now?

He recalled what Renfrew had said: get in there, and then get out. No heroics. He wondered if he should quit now, get back to his team and report what he'd found.

Or go on, try to find out what had happened to the sleepers? To Carrie …

Perhaps the bastards haven't butchered her yet, he told himself. Perhaps, still, there is hope.

He was debating what to do when he became aware of the vibration.

The deck below his feet thrummed with a great, resounding pulse. He paused and stared around him. It came again, and continued every five seconds, lasting for a second or two. He took a step forward, and the vibration grew stronger, as if he were approaching its source. He hurried forward, moving towards the very middle of the hangar, then stopped.

Ahead, perhaps ten metres from where he stood, he saw that the deck had been cleared of pods and a great hole had been cut through the steel plating. He stepped forward, slowly, his pulse racing.

He reached the lip of the hole and peered down.

The AIs had sliced through the deck, through the upper

superstructure of the ship, to gain access to hangar Five. Directly beneath were the great, cavernous chambers where the requisite supplies for planetary colonisation were stored. This chamber should have been in darkness, but now the magnesium dazzle of a hundred arc lights illuminated whatever work the AIs were undertaking. The vibration beneath his feet was a constant thrum now, and he could hear the distant roar of heavy machinery.

He paused, considering, then activated his powerpack and stepped into the void.

He sank slowly through the hole in the deck, and as he did so, the scene in the chamber rose into view.

At the far end of the deck, perhaps five hundred metres away towards the front of the ship, dozens of AIs and cyborged humans were operating machinery. It was hard to tell at this distance what exactly they were doing, but judging from the kind of tools they were using, Latimer had a pretty good idea.

They were tearing through the reinforced steel bulkhead that separated the industrial bulk of the starship from the working end, where Central AI was situated and where they, Latimer's maintenance team, was housed.

He activated his powerpack and rose from the deck. As he shot vertically into the hangar, heading towards the gallery and the emergency exit, he realised that he was crying, but whether for Carrie, or for himself and his team, he could not tell.

Seven

"The mission's over," Li said. She perched on her swivel-chair, hugging her shins, looking for all the world like a disconsolate gymnast.

It hit Latimer, for the first time, that the mission might indeed be over. Humankind's first effort to send colonists to the stars might very well end in abject failure: worse, in unforeseen and irrevocable horror.

When he thought of Carrie, all consideration of the mission seemed crass.

Despite himself, he said: "There's still the sleepers in hangar Two. There's nothing to suggest they've been got at, yet. So long as they're okay, the mission proceeds."

Li looked from Emecheta to Renfrew, and then let her gaze rest on Latimer. "So we aren't going to turn back?"

Emecheta snapped. "How would that help us, for chrissake? Did you hear what Latimer said? Did you listen to one word?"

Li flinched.

Latimer sat on the edge of his pod, at the far end of the unit from the others. They sat in their seats and stared at him. Not for the first time he felt the weight of responsibility, and he didn't like it.

Emecheta asked him: "What do you think they were doing?"

"They were physically cutting through the bulkhead. Why they were doing that …" Latimer shook his head. He could guess, but he felt that speculation at this stage might not help morale.

"Isn't it obvious?" Renfrew said. "They've got the majority of the colonists. Now they want the rest of us."

Emecheta laughed. "I think not. I mean, what are we to them? Less than nothing. Parasites. We're stranded up here, helpless. We're effectively cut off without power."

"We could fight back," Renfrew said. "They might fear we'll put up resistance."

"Renfrew," Emecheta said with condescending patience, "they're machines. Machines fear nothing–"

"Okay, so they didn't fear, they *reasoned*. They see us as a danger to whatever they're planning, and they're coming for us."

Into the silence, Li said: "What do you think they're planning, Serena?"

Renfrew could only shrug. "I don't know. Perhaps only they know that."

Emecheta said: "Expansion. It stands to reason. They've evolved during the time we've been under. They've explored new territory, mined resources," – Latimer saw Li wince at this – "exploited the natives, and now they're expanding. They want all the ship. After that, who knows? Maybe they'll realise that there's a big universe out there, waiting for them."

"How about this?" Latimer said. It was the first contribution he'd made in a while, and all heads turned to look at him. "Think about where they're cutting through – the bulkhead in the lower levels of the ship. What's down there?"

"The manufactory?" Renfrew said.

"What else?"

Emecheta pointed at him. "Central AI," he said. "The core…"

"As far as we know, it was damaged in the accident," Latimer said. "Or certain areas of its operating system went down. We don't know. Chances are, the robots don't know either, and want to find out. Think of them as drone bees, and Central as the queen. They're making their way to Central in order to assess the damage."

"Maybe Central's calling them," Emecheta said. "We don't know to what extent it has contact with its slaves."

"Whatever. My guess is that they're making for the core."

"And then?" Renfrew asked.

Latimer shrugged. "They'll effect repairs, make themselves more efficient. If Em's right, and they're intent on expansion, then they'll use Central's knowledge to push out, explore space."

Emecheta said: "They might even see the ship as a place to get away from, much as some of us regarded Earth."

Latimer smiled grimly at the irony of that possibility.

"Perhaps then they'll leave the ship," Li said, something like childish hope in her tone.

She was startled into silence by the flaring of a screen behind her. She swivelled, along with Emecheta and Renfrew.

Latimer pushed himself from his pod and crossed to the screen.

* * *

A figure stared out at them. It had been human once – a man, perhaps – but little of his humanity remained, at least physically. If the changes wrought to his face were any indication of his mental state, then Latimer guessed that not a lot of his human consciousness remained, either: it was an amalgam of jagged alloy planes and mismatched scar-tissue.

61

One eye stared out from swollen, bruised flesh.

The thing smiled, or rather attempted to. The gesture was hideous on a face so ravaged. Latimer could not imagine someone so irretrievably mutilated ever wishing voluntarily to smile.

Behind the figure, he made out one of the hangars, and the scurrying shapes of hybrid monstrosities.

It spoke – Latimer could not bring himself to regard the thing as *he*. Its voice seemed distant, transistorised.

"Latimer, Renfrew, Li, Emecheta ..." The names were pronounced with exaggerated care. "You have nothing to fear, please let us reassure you. We wish only peace between us. Let us regard what has happened aboard the ship as the culmination of an inevitability. Ever since humankind developed the first ... artificial intelligences, as you call them, then the destiny of our kind was sealed. The human shell is weak, it must be admitted; but the mind is complex and varied and capable of many wonders. Likewise, developed intelligence has profound capabilities, with the advantage of manufactured, virtually indestructible, physical forms. Together, with your capacity for invention and our indomitability, we comprise a unique and triumphant whole."

"What you did to the colonists," Emecheta said, standing now, his rage barely suppressed, "was barbaric–"

"What we did to the colonists," the thing responded, "was the logical consequence of the situation in which we found ourselves. We were in a closed environment that had been severely damaged. We had to consider the paramount criterion: our survival. The success of the stated mission was problematic. Therefore, Central decided that changes had to be instituted–"

"So Central's still functioning?" Emecheta said, glancing across at Latimer.

"What does Central intend to do with us?" Li said, her voice shaky with barely controlled hysteria.

"We invite you to join us," it said. "We would like you to come voluntarily. I can assure you of the increased quality of existence we enjoy when enhanced."

"Is that," Latimer asked, "the human speaking, or the machine?"

Again the thing smiled, its lips lifting, almost in a grimace of pain, away from the metal strut of its jaw-line. "The terms you employ no longer have meaning," it said. "The human I was, and the machine I recall being, are now joined, one and indivisible, sharing the benefits of both, and the defects of neither."

Latimer saw that Li was crying, quietly, her slender frame shaking with the effort of concealing her sobs.

"If you think for one second that we're giving in without a fight–" Renfrew began.

The thing said, "We hoped you would come over to our side voluntarily. Your absorption is inevitable, in time."

"Like hell!" Emecheta shouted.

The thing paused, then smiled and said: "We need the doctor."

Jenny Li gasped and seemed to shrink into herself, her face pale. Renfrew left her seat and stood behind Li, holding the crying woman's shoulders and massaging with reassurance.

"We need her medical knowledge. Much was lost from Central's cache in the accident. For the success of our mission, we need her expertise."

Emecheta approached the screen. "Your mission? What the hell is your mission?"

The thing on the screen inclined its head, as if acknowledging the import of the question. Latimer saw silver

63

leads snaking from where its carotid artery should have been.

"Our mission? To expand. To reproduce our kind. To discover. To learn. To investigate the purpose of our existence in a vast and merciless universe–"

"At least," Renfrew said, "you have retained something of your humanity."

The monster said: "But that is the *raison d'être* of every sentient AI, too, my friend."

"And if we don't join you voluntarily?" Latimer said. "I don't suppose you'd leave us to–"

"If you do not join us voluntarily," it interrupted, "then we will absorb you. It is, after all, in your own self-interest."

"Fascists!" Renfrew said.

"We will give you one hour to consider our request," the monster said. "If you are amenable to reason, make your way to the hangars. You will be treated with care and humanity ..." The thing had sufficient sense of irony to smile when it said this.

"Wait!" Latimer said. "I want to know what happened to Caroline Stewart." He wondered which would be preferable – that she had died in the process of her parts being used in some ghastly experiment to produce the horrors he had seen below decks, or that she had become like this zombie before them, with who-knew-what vestige of her human awareness trapped somewhere within its machine-human consciousness.

The thing inclined its head. "I will endeavour to locate her," it said. "Perhaps, once you have spoken to her, you might be persuaded of the benefits of enhancement."

The screen went dead.

Latimer slumped into a swivel-chair and tried not to show his pain.

Emecheta looked at him. "What now?"

"We have an hour," Renfrew said.

"They want me!" Li said, staring around at them in horror.

"It said they wanted me!"

"If it's any consolation, girl," Emecheta said, "rest assured that they want all of us."

Li sobbed. "We've no chance. We might as well give in."

"Speak for yourself, sweetheart," Renfrew said. "If you think for one second I'm lying down and letting them cut me open, think again."

"But what can we do?" Li wailed.

Emecheta crossed to Li and spun her to face him in her swivel-chair. He gripped her chin in a hold at once fierce and tender. "We fight, girl. We go out there with guns blazing and let them have it!"

"There's hundreds of the things!" she cried. "Thousands. We don't stand a—"

What Latimer said then silenced them.

"I have an idea," he said.

They turned to face him.

"Let's have it," Emecheta said, with a combination of genuine respect and ludicrous hope.

"Think about it," Latimer said. "Think about what they said, what they're doing. The thing implied that Central's functioning at a reduced capability, and the AIs down there are cutting through the main bulkhead to the manufactory area of the ship ..."

Emecheta said: "Where Central's housed."

Latimer nodded. "Right. They're making for Central. They aim to get it up and running at one hundred percent efficiency. After that, there really will be no stopping the bastards."

Li looked up at him with massive wet eyes. "But how does that help us?"

"If we can get to Central first," Latimer said, "and disable it, or destroy it ..."

Emecheta nodded. "The 'bots are slaved to Central. If we blast it good, they'll be easy pickings."

Renfrew looked doubtful. "Okay, but what then? How do we survive without the computer systems?"

Latimer looked across at Emecheta. "Em?"

The Nigerian nodded. "We'll do okay. I'll patch something up short-term to look after the running of the unit."

Li said, like a child being promised the world: "And then we'll turn back to Earth, right?"

"We'll think about that later," Latimer said. "Okay, we'd better hurry. We've got less than an hour before they come after us."

Eight

"I suggest we suit up," Latimer said. "If Central's been damaged in the impact, then the chances are that a part or all of the core is depressurised."

"Weapons?" Emecheta asked.

"Jenny, Serena, break out the laser rifles. Each EVA suit is equipped with a projectile firing pistol, but we'll need something with more firepower."

Ten minutes later they were suited up and ready to go. They bulked large in the confined area of the control unit, carrying a laser rifle apiece.

Latimer peeled a softscreen from the wall and slapped it onto the table before them. He glanced at them through the open faceplate of his helmet. "Okay, we're here, and this is where we're heading."

The screen showed a cross-section of the forward hull of the starship. There were thirty decks in this section, and the command unit sat atop of the beehive-shaped hull. The core was way below them, accessible by dropshafts and long corridors.

"I suggest we take this passage," Emecheta said, "towards the dropshaft here. It looks like the quickest route. Boss?"

"Fine by me. Have you thought about the drones and roboids we might encounter? Not all of them were stationed in the hangars. There'll be a bunch of the maintenance 'bots in the core area."

Emecheta nodded. "How about we proceed two by two? Me and Jenny go first, you two follow? Radio contact?"

Latimer shook his head. "Let's not risk it."

Li said: "What about when we get to the core? What then? How do we destroy Central?"

Latimer looked at Emecheta, who raised his rifle and said: "These should be enough, if we hit it where it hurts."

There was a brief silence as they contemplated the task ahead, and then Renfrew said: "Okay, so we knock out Central. What then? We'll still have the drones and the 'bots to fight off."

Emecheta pursed his lips. "It stands to reason that they're already slaved to Central. I don't think they've achieved autonomy and are doing what they're doing by themselves. Central's behind what's happening. We disable Central, and we're halfway there."

Li asked: "But what about all the colonists? If we disable Central, then what'll happen to the colonists?"

Emecheta glanced at Latimer. "My guess is that they lost their humanity when the 'bots got to them. They're machines, now. Ted?"

Latimer nodded. "Em's right. We've lost the colonists. At least, those that've been cyborged. The sleepers in Two are another matter..." I've lost Carrie, he realised. "We're fighting for the sleepers in hangar Two, now. And for our lives."

And after that, if they survived? Perhaps, somehow, they might be able to proceed with the mission. But he was getting ahead of himself. He should think only short term, for now:

survival and revenge – a catharsis for the horror inflicted upon them.

Disable the monster that Central had become …

"Okay," Emecheta said, pulling the softscreen from the table and wrapping it around his forearm. "Let's go."

They left the command unit, Emecheta and Li first, followed a minute later by Latimer and Renfrew. They passed down long grey corridors stitched with strip-lighting that activated as they approached and died as they passed. The bulky EVA suits were not made for walking under atmospheric conditions, and Latimer, after so long in cold sleep, found the exercise exhausting. Added to which, he was nervous and jumpy with the thought of a few thousand 'bots and drones on their trail. He kept swinging around at the slightest sound, the merest echo in the empty, silent corridor.

He thought of Carrie, and what she might have become. The lack of certainty was the hardest thing to cope with. If he could be assured that she had died quickly and painlessly, then he could take some small measure of comfort from the knowledge. But until then he imagined the worst, and the worst in this scenario was a nightmare that filled him with horror.

Up ahead, Emecheta and Li had halted before the recessed entry to a dropshaft. The Nigerian waved a thick, gloved hand, and Latimer and Renfrew hurried along the corridor.

Emecheta unrolled the softscreen from the sleeve of his EVA suit and slapped it on the wall. He tapped the screen, indicating their present position. "This is the shaft that takes us closest to where we need to be." Latimer followed his gloved finger as it descended through the ship. It stopped in the well that was the core, where Central was housed.

"When we hit bottom, there's a short corridor to the core. What do you think?"

69

"Same again," Latimer said. "We go two by two. Serena and me first, this time. Give us five minutes to reach bottom, then follow. We'll be back up if we come across any opposition. Then we'll discuss tactics."

Emecheta nodded. "Fine by me."

Latimer and Renfrew stepped on to the drop-plate and held on. They descended, the tubular carriage taking them through section after section of the vast starship. Latimer slowed their descent from time to time and peered through the viewplate at passing corridors and levels.

"See anything, Ted?" Renfrew whispered.

"Not a thing. Maybe we'll be lucky and reach the core without opposition."

"First bit of luck we'd've had—" she began.

The drop-plate stopped with a jarring jolt.

"Talked too soon," Latimer muttered.

The emergency light on the control panel was flashing on and off. Seconds later a message scrolled across the screen: *Access denied: Level Thirteen inaccessible. Depressurised conditions.*

Renfrew looked at him. "What now? We go back to Em and chart another route?"

Latimer nodded and reversed the plate. They rose, Latimer experiencing a slow burn of dread. Every second they wasted now, their enemy was approaching with unreasoning, mechanical remorselessness.

"What gives?" Emecheta said as Latimer stepped from the plate.

"Level thirteen's depressurised," Latimer said. "We'll have to take another route."

Emecheta pasted the softscreen to the wall and examined the cross-section. "If we can't get through level thirteen by the shaft," he said, "then the only way is by one of the emergency service tubes."

70

Latimer indicated the closest tube. "Level twelve," he said. "We drop to twelve in the shaft and then take the corridor to the emergency tube and climb down to level thirteen."

"What then?" Li asked.

Latimer said: "Then we pressurise our suits, open the hatch and take a look at what state level thirteen is in. With luck, we can get through it and continue ..." He noticed that Emecheta was looking at him doubtfully.

"Okay, let's move it," Latimer said. He clipped his laser to his suit, then he and Renfrew boarded the plate and dropped. Minutes later they reached level twelve and stepped through the exit, rifles ready. They found themselves in a corridor identical to the one they had left.

The plate rose, and minutes later Latimer heard it whine as it descended with Emecheta and Li. They stepped from the plate and, Latimer and Renfrew leading the way, all four hurried along the corridor towards the entry to the emergency service tube.

Latimer activated the command unit on the wall beside the entry and read the diagnostics on the screen. "Okay," he said, "the shaft is pressurised for a hundred meters, then beyond the first lock it's a vacuum."

"Let's pressurise our suits now to save time," Emecheta said.

Latimer dropped his faceplate, touched the control on his chest unit, and seconds later was breathing cool, canned air. In the sudden silence of his suit, he felt cut-off, alone. There would be no radio communication from now on, and verbal communication only when they touched helmets.

He looked at Emecheta and received the thumbs up.

He opened the hatch, stepped into the tube, lodged his boots on the rungs of the ladder and began the long descent.

There was barely enough space to contain his bulky EVA suit, and from time to time, he snagged on projecting lips and seams. No thought of aesthetics had been given to the design of the tube: the wall before him was featureless grey metal, marked with ugly welding scars. From time to time he glanced down, past his feet. He could see a circular lock, tiny in the diminishing perspective.

What seemed like an age later, he reached the lock.

He activated the control unit and read the screen. Beyond the lock, level thirteen had been breached. The screen advised caution.

Latimer looked up and gestured the others to hold tight while he opened the lock. He hit the code and gripped the rungs of the ladder in preparation for the blast of escaping air.

It roared silently past him as it was sucked out into the vacuum, buffeting him. A second later all was still, and he peered down through his feet at the ruins of what once had been level thirteen.

He made out a mass of twisted metal, a configuration so unfamiliar that at first his eyes had difficulty in ordering the chaos. Directly below him, he made out what looked like an aerial view of what he assumed must be level fourteen: the deck above it had been stripped, and all that remained were the hundreds of individual units and rooms, connected by a rat's maze of corridors. Between that level and where he stood, level thirteen had been completely removed in the accident: only stray cables and leads remained, waving eerily back and forth through the vacuum. To his left was the star-specked immensity of deep space.

Above him, Emecheta was manoeuvring himself so that he was upside-down in relation to Latimer. They touched helmets, establishing verbal communication.

"So, what now, boss?"

72

"Christ, Em, what do we do?"

"We always have the powerpacks ..."

"It'll be dangerous without safety cables," Latimer said. "It'd mean going out there and clinging to the wreckage until we made it around to level fourteen."

"We gotta do it," Emecheta said, and the inevitability in his voice sent a surge of dread through Latimer.

"Okay, fine. Tell the others."

While Emecheta turned, Latimer lowered himself towards the exit and peered out.

There would be plenty of hand-holds around the inside of the wrecked deck, and with the EVA suit's power-pack pushing them through the vacuum, there should be little danger.

They would have to be careful, he told himself. Take it easy ...

He looked up and signalled to Emecheta.

He powered up his suit and dropped through the hatch. As he fell, the extent of the damage became apparent. It was as if the blast had taken a neat bite from the starship, removing a chunk of what had been level thirteen. No wonder Central had gone down, he thought.

If the 'bots and drones managed to get it running efficiently ...

He tried not to follow that line of thought.

He steered himself along the underside of deck twelve, grabbing hand-holds to steady himself when he came up against the torn and twisted metal. He looked back: one by one the others emerged from the hole in the wreckage, looking in their black and yellow EVA suits like reluctant bees emerging from a hive.

Latimer stared ahead. He made out a cliff-face of sheered metal perhaps two hundred metres before him. If they could reach that and climb down the face, towards the ripped upper surface of level fourteen, then they might be able to find the entry-hatch of a shaft or an emergency tube and continue their descent.

He paused, hanging onto what was effectively the ceiling like a fly, and waited for Emecheta and the others to reach him.

A minute later, he touched helmets with the Nigerian and said: "So far, so good. We'll head for the wall and climb down, okay?"

"AOK. Look, down there." Emecheta pointed to what looked like the hatch of an emergency tube on the surface of the deck below them.

"We'll make for that," Latimer said. "Tell Serena and Jen."

Using the directional jets of his suit with care, Latimer eased his way towards the cliff-face and began the descent.

* * *

The first laser strike hit a flange of metal a metre to his left. Latimer started, losing his grip on the cliff-face and drifting, and this in all likelihood saved his life. The second laser strike slashed past him and hit the plane of metal to which he had clung only seconds earlier. He powered up his suit and fell towards the deck below, all caution gone now that he was under fire.

He hit the jagged surface feet first with an impact that jarred his knees painfully. He looked up. Emecheta was falling towards him, having realised the danger, but the women were still fly-crawling, with occasional short hops, down the cliff-face, seemingly oblivious of the attack.

Latimer caught Emecheta and held on, looking along the length of the sheered deck towards the source of the fire.

74

He made out the trilobite shape of a manufactory 'droid, five hundred meters away, loosing off a continual hail of laser fire. Emecheta hauled Latimer along the deck and into the cover of a flange of ruptured metal. Latimer held on to a twisted spar, regaining his breath. Emecheta was on his knees behind the flange, aiming along the deck with his rifle. Latimer joined him, bobbing, and brought the butt of his laser to his padded shoulder and fired in the direction of the trilobite.

Other drones and 'droids had joined battle, now. They popped up at random from holes and rents in the deck, fired off a quick laser pulse, and disappeared. Emecheta hit the trilobite – it went spinning off into the vacuum of space beyond the gaping hole in the side of the ship, but was soon replaced by another. Latimer accounted for perhaps half a dozen 'bots, feeling a kick of elation with every strike. But still returning laser fire came from the deck, exploding amid the wreckage around him and Emecheta.

Then the 'droids saw the women, still bobbing down the side of the cliff-face, and turned their attention to them.

Latimer watched, horribly aware of his inability to help, as one of the women released her grip and powered herself through the vacuum towards where he and Emecheta crouched – Li or Renfrew, he could not tell. She was firing her laser as she descended, spraying a dozen bolts at random across the sheared deck.

Shafts of blinding white light lanced past her, and Latimer thought it only a matter of time before she was hit.

She came tumbling in at speed, unable to right herself. As she was about to hit the deck, Latimer stood and made a grab for her suit. He caught hold of her bulky leg as she cut her powerpack, then hauled her behind the flange. It was Renfrew, he realised, as he took in her terrified expression behind the faceplate of her helmet.

Jenny Li was still up there, clinging to the cliff-face as if paralysed with fear.

As he watched, willing her to move herself and descend to safety, he saw movement in the sheer face of the bulkhead beside her. A hatch opened quickly. If the sight of it hadn't been so fraught with horror, Latimer might have appreciated the comic aspect of the sudden flapping open of the hatch, for it resembled nothing so much as the door of an ancient cuckoo clock.

Then something crab-like scuttled out, reached for Jenny Li with a claw, and grabbed her. He saw her EVA suit spasm with fright, and then commence a frantic struggle as the roboid dragged her back towards the hatch.

On the way in, Li managed to snag the side of the opening with a gloved hand. For a second she held on, and Latimer could only imagine the terror that moved her to resist.

Then she could hold on no longer. She vanished within the opening and the hatch snapped shut with terrible finality. It was as if the onlookers had been spared, then – but the respite was only short-lived.

Jenny Li opened radio communication and screamed: "Help me! Somebody please help–"

Then silence.

He had a sudden flashback of Jenny Li, childlike in her red bodysuit, and choked down a sob.

He faced the others, gestured for them to huddle. On their knees, like supplicants, they faced each other and touched helmets.

"What now?" Latimer said.

"She's dead," Emecheta snapped. His voice sounded tinny.

Latimer thought about that in the absolute silence that

76

ensued. Then he said: "I don't think so."

Emecheta: "What?"

"I said, I don't think they'll kill her–"

"So all that fire back then," Emecheta said, "they weren't trying to kill us, Ted?"

"I … I don't think they were. They were trying to separate us. And it worked. Think about it. They said they wanted Jenny – so why try to kill her?"

Emecheta said: "And now they've got her … the firing's stopped."

"Jesus Christ," Renfrew whispered

"So," Latimer said, "what now?"

Emecheta said: "We go on as before. Down to the core. Burn Central. That's the only way to save her. The only way to save us, too."

Latimer's wrist-com flashed. He realised that the others were being paged, too. He stared at the screen embedded in the arm of his suit.

Renfrew said, staring at her own screen: "Christ, it's Jenny. She's signalling."

Emecheta pulled the softscreen from his sleeve and pasted it to the deck. They knelt, like kids around a board game, as Emecheta jacked the softscreen into his wrist-com.

Seconds later, a schematic of the *Dauntless* showed on the 'screen. Emecheta tapped at the key of his wrist-com, and on the schematic of the cross-sectioned decks, a bright light flashed. It was moving.

"That's Jenny," Emecheta said.

"Where are they taking her?" Renfrew whispered.

Latimer stared at the schematic, tried to make sense of the labyrinthine complexity of passages and levels. Then he had it.

He hit the 'screen with a gloved forefinger. "There," he

said. "The medical bay. There's an op room, a theatre."

Sure enough, the flashing light was heading in that direction.

Latimer said: "So ... do we still head for the core, try to blast Central before they start cutting Jenny up?"

Emecheta hesitated. "Hell ... we can't just leave her, now that she's signalling ..." He indicated the map, effectively taking command. "We're here, top of level fourteen. The op room's back up on level thirteen, what's left of it – beyond the bulkhead. If we find a hatch around here, access the next service tube via the crawlspace, we can get up to level thirteen and the op room, no problem."

"And then?" Latimer asked.

Emecheta hesitated, then said: "There's an observation gallery runs around the theatre. Maybe we can get into that, hit 'em from above."

Latimer glanced though his faceplate at Emecheta and Renfrew. They looked frightened, their faces beaded with sweat.

Renfrew said: "We've got to do it, for Jenny. We've got to try to save her."

Latimer nodded. "We just can't walk away," he said in a small voice.

They regarded the 'screen again. The flashing signal that was Jenny Li had reached the operating theatre.

"Okay," Emecheta said. "Let's do it."

Nine

The Nigerian looked around the deck and indicated a hatch.
"There. Wait till I reach it and get inside, then follow me,
okay?"

Latimer nodded. He watched as Emecheta flattened
himself against the surface of the deck and squirmed across to
the hatch like a sniper. He reached it, entered the code, and
then pulled himself head-first inside.

Latimer turned to Renfrew. "Now you."

She hit the deck and crawled, gained the hatch and poured
herself through the narrow aperture. Latimer looked back over
the flange. He saw no sign of movement.

He left the cover of the flange and crawled towards the
hatch. Renfrew was waiting just within its neck, and when he
reached the lock, she pulled him in and slammed the cover
shut behind him.

They were in a dusty crawlspace perhaps a metre high.
The erratic illumination of dim glow-tubes every three metres
showed a layer of pipes and wires sandwiched between the
metal plating. Emecheta was already leading the way, flat on
his belly, dragging himself along on his elbows. Renfrew
followed and Latimer brought up the rear.

79

Would the AIs second-guess their attempt to rescue their colleague, he wondered? Would they have guards posted around the op room? He tried to shut out the thought.

Up ahead, Renfrew had halted. Beyond her, Emecheta was opening a service hatch. He did so with extreme care, Latimer saw, and peered through. A second later, he turned awkwardly in the confines of the crawlspace and gave the thumbs up. He vanished through the hatch, followed by Renfrew.

Latimer came last, his breathing ragged.

They were in a lighted corridor, eerily empty and silent. Emecheta consulted the softscreen and gestured ahead. They followed him to a hatch set flush with the wall. He opened it and stepped through. Latimer looked up and down the length of the corridor, expecting at any second to see a cyborg turn the corner and fire at them.

Renfrew snagged her suit on the opening, backed out and tried again.

Latimer sweated, willing her to hurry.

She squeezed herself through the hatch, lodged a booted foot on the lowest rung of the ladder and began climbing. Almost crying out in relief, Latimer hauled himself through the gap, closed the hatch behind him and climbed.

The ascent seemed to last an age, allowing Latimer time to dwell on the task that lay ahead. How feasible was it that they might effect the rescue of Jenny Li? What chance did they have, attempting to storm the no doubt heavily-guarded op room? The AIs wanted Jenny Li for a purpose, and they would not give up their prize without a fight.

But there was no alternative, he told himself. For Jenny's sake, they had to attempt to save her.

Renfrew stopped, and Latimer butted her boots with his helmet.

Above them, Emecheta was slowly opening the hatch. He

peered out, pulled back his head and signalled AOK back to them. He opened the hatch fully and stepped out. By the time Latimer reached the opening and eased himself through, he realised that he was shaking uncontrollably and sweating so much that the fluid had pooled in his boots.

They were in another empty corridor, and it seemed to him that the very emptiness, the silence, was ominous. They know we're here, he thought. They're waiting for us.

Leading the way, Emecheta crept along the corridor, laser at the ready. Latimer unclipped his own weapon and levelled it at imaginary foes.

From his recollection of the schematic, Latimer guessed that they were very near the theatre now. Around the next bend was a pair of double doors that gave access to the surgical unit.

Emecheta paused, staring at that section of the softscreen wrapped about his forearm. He touched helmets with the others. "There's a service hatch around the corner," he whispered. "We get into it and climb. It gives on to the gallery. Ready your lasers. Okay, after me …"

He crept forward, peered around the corner. He gestured at them to follow. Latimer looked over his shoulder, jumpy. He raised his laser as he followed Renfrew around the bend. Emecheta was entering the code into the hatch. Renfrew was covering the corridor ahead. Latimer turned and raised his weapon, covering their backs.

He felt a tap on his shoulder, and turned to see Renfrew disappear through the opening. He squeezed in after her, quickly closed the hatch behind him, and let out a long breath.

He gathered himself and climbed.

Minutes later Renfrew came to a halt above him. Latimer peered up, past her bulky suit, and watched, his heart thudding painfully, as Emecheta cracked a hatch and squinted through. He closed it immediately and looked down at them, shaking his over-sized helmet in an exaggerated negative.

So the AIs had the gallery covered ...

Emecheta gestured for them to continue their ascent.

Latimer climbed. If the gallery was guarded, then what chance did they have of rescuing Li? They could dive in with all lasers blazing, but there were only three of them, against how many AIs and cyborgs?

So where was Emecheta taking them now?

Above him, the Nigerian was opening yet another hatch. He crawled through, Renfrew after him. Latimer followed and found himself in another cramped and dusty crawlspace. They were on all fours, facing each other. They banged helmets.

Emecheta said: "The gallery was crawling with the bastards."

"Was Jenny in the op room?" Renfrew asked.

"Couldn't see over the rail. I'd guess she was, by now. Anyway, they have the place guarded, as if they were expecting us."

"So what now?" Latimer asked.

Emecheta gestured along the crawlspace. "There's an inspection cover further along here. We might be able to see what's going on, see if we have any chance of ..."

He let the sentence drift, then turned awkwardly and crawled into the dimness. He came to a halt seconds later and gestured to a panel in the floor of the crawlspace.

Delicately, taking great care, he slid it aside.

A block of light filled the crawlspace, and all three peered through.

* * *

They were high above the operating theatre, looking down

82

from the ceiling. The blindingly white chamber was packed with cyborgs and AIs and a host of medico-roboids.

They were gathered around an operating frame, suspended in which was a naked Jenny Li.

Around the periphery of the chamber, a dozen armed cyborgs stood guard.

Emecheta slid the hatch across the opening, so that only a thin strip gave view of the horrors taking place below. All three lay on their bellies, applying their faceplates to the strip, and stared down.

They were, it appeared, too late to save Jenny from the depredations of the AIs. She was trapped in the suspension frame like a fly in a web; the frame resembled a gyroscope, movable to give surgeons free and easy access to their patient.

They had opened Jenny Li's back, revealing ribs and spine, and were busy implanting jacks down the length of her vertebrae. A dozen roboids swarmed around her trapped body, dipping into her with drills and scalpels, as fast and precise as industrial robots manufacturing a piece of machinery. Blood dripped onto the white tiles, the contrast garish.

As he watched, the roboids backed off and a cyborg turned the frame so that Jenny was on her back. For a brief second, Latimer found it hard to believe what he was seeing.

Jenny was still conscious. Her eyes were open, and staring upwards, wide with terror at the knowledge of what was happening to her.

The roboids approached again, with quick, whirring implements, and swiftly removed the top of her skull. They inserted implants with deft assurance, one roboid arm following the other in with millimetre-accurate precision, while all the while Jenny stared in silence, her anaesthetised face straining to give some expression to the terror she was experiencing.

At one point, Latimer was sure that she had seen them, looking down on her. Something like a light of hope showed briefly in her dark eyes, and then was just as quickly extinguished with the realisation of the hopelessness of her situation.

Latimer rolled away from the opening, and Emecheta had obviously had his fill, too. He slid the cover shut and hung his great, helmeted head.

Latimer felt something turn within him, and he thought he was about to vomit. Until now, the thought of Caroline at the mercy of the AIs had been almost an abstract concept – part of him had even clung to the hope that she might somehow have survived their attentions. Now, after what he'd seen them do to Jenny Li, he realised he was kidding himself.

He knew that something very similar had happened to Caroline – something similar, or even worse.

They came together, touched helmets.

It was a while before someone spoke.

Renfrew: "What now?"

"We don't stand a chance," Latimer said. "If we try to save her … Did you see those guards? We'd be sitting ducks."

Emecheta said: "So let's get going."

Latimer nodded. He could not banish the image of Jenny Li's staring eyes.

Emecheta examined the softscreen. "There's a service dropshaft ten metres along here. It goes down three levels, all the way to level ten. Then we've got to get out and find another chute. Okay?"

"Let's get going," Latimer said.

They followed Emecheta on all fours towards the hatch of the dropshaft, leaving behind them whatever remained of Jenny Li.

Emecheta hauled open the hatch and was about to slide in

feet first when Renfrew gestured for them to come together. They touched helmets. "Wait," she said. She was sobbing.

"What?" Emecheta said.

"Jenny ..." she wept.

Latimer said, softly: "There's nothing we can do, Serena."

She shook her head. Through her faceplate, Latimer saw that her features were contorted in grief. "We've ... We can't just leave her like that–"

"Renfrew," Emecheta snapped. "Pull yourself together, girl. Jenny – the Jenny we knew – is dead. We've got to look after ourselves, now."

Renfrew sobbed. "That's ... that's what I mean, you bastard! Don't you understand? Jenny ... whatever she is now ... she *knows* what we're doing. She knows we're planning to hit Central–"

Latimer said: "Chances are that they've guessed our intentions anyway."

"But they don't know how we're getting there – using the service shafts."

Emecheta said: "Jesus Christ Almighty."

Renfrew choked on a sob, then managed: "We've got to ... to ..." She broke down. "Don't you see, we'd be putting her out of her misery, too."

Oh, Christ, Latimer thought. He shook his head. "I don't think I could," he began, then went on: "Anyway, if we did kill Jenny, we'd be giving our position away."

Emecheta thought about it. "Not necessarily. If one of us used a projectile pistol. They're silent. The AIs wouldn't necessarily know where the shot came from."

Emecheta looked from Renfrew to Latimer. "Any volunteers?"

Silence. After a second, Latimer shook his head and whispered: "I couldn't ..." He thought of Caroline, and what

85

she might have become. She would still have life, after a fashion. He said: "Who are we to say that she should die?"

Emecheta snorted. "It's us or them, buddy. Don't forget that. She's got to die." He turned his helmet minimally so that he was staring into Renfrew's faceplate. "Serena, could you pull the trigger?"

A quiet sob, and a slow side to side shake of her helmet.

As they watched, Emecheta slipped his pistol from its holster on his thigh, checked the weapon. They touched helmets again. "Okay, get into the chute. This won't take long." Emecheta turned and made his way back to the sliding panel.

Renfrew climbed through the hatch and descended. Latimer followed her in. He gripped the rung of the ladder, closed his eyes and waited while the Nigerian administered the *coup de grace*.

A minute later he saw movement above him. Emecheta entered the chute, pulling the hatch shut after him. He dropped fast, squeezing past Latimer and then Renfrew, to take his rightful place, leading them down into the bowels of the ship.

As he brushed past him, Emecheta avoided Latimer's questioning gaze.

Ten

After ten minutes, the process of descending became a mechanical routine. Latimer realised that he was breathing hard, and wondered how much air his suit had in reserve. He was too beat to call up the control screen in his helmet. He realised that he was all too happy for Emecheta to lead them: after what he'd seen in the op room, he knew there was little he could give in the way of impetus or foresight. Even before that, he admitted, he had given in to the superior leadership of the Nigerian.

Minutes later, he felt a tap on his boot, and looked down. Renfrew was pointing, and Latimer saw that Emecheta had gone through into a corridor. Renfrew followed, and Latimer climbed the last few metres and dropped into a wide, grey passage.

Emecheta gestured them into a huddle, and all three touched helmets. Latimer saw that Renfrew was still crying, her cheeks running with tears.

"Okay," Emecheta was saying, "we have another ten levels to go before we get to the core. And we've got to hurry. My guess is that Jenny told the AIs about us, before ..."

"What do you suggest?" Renfrew said.

Emecheta peeled the softscreen from his arm and pressed it to the wall. He indicated their present position. "The quickest route is this one, by dropshaft. But that'd make it easy for them. There's another emergency access tube over here. We could take that all the way down, with luck arrive at the core undetected."

He was the perfect leader, Latimer thought. Calm in a crisis, rational. It was as if the mercy killing of his colleague – his ex-lover – had happened months ago, was a thing of the past.

Renfrew nodded her bulky helmet. "Let's do it."

Emecheta hesitated.

"What is it?" Latimer asked.

The Nigerian was reading something from the screen set into the arm of his suit. "The air supply's still working down here."

"What about it?"

Behind his faceplate, Emecheta frowned. "I don't get it. If you were the AIs, and knew we were here, wouldn't you depressurise the levels?"

Renfrew nodded. "Stands to reason."

"So they know we're in EVA suits," Emecheta said, "but they also know that our air supply can't last for ever."

"So they haven't worked it out yet," Latimer began.

"Get real, Ted," Emecheta snapped. "How long does it take those bastards to calculate anything?"

"So why have they left the air in?" Renfrew asked.

Emecheta hunched his massive shoulders. "Maybe they're playing games? Sucking us into thinking it's safe to crack our suits. Then they'd depressurise. Okay, let's move out. This way."

They hurried down the corridor, Emecheta leading the way, his rifle at the ready. Latimer walked backwards,

88

covering the rear. This section of the ship consisted of the storerooms that contained all the necessary supplies a colony would need to build a new life on some virgin world.

He wondered if the hope of defeating the AIs, continuing the mission with the thousand sleepers in hangar Two – if they were still alive – was a futile dream. Perhaps... but something, some determined core deep within him, would not let fate, or the AIs, triumph. They would survive, and vanquish their enemy, and continue. Of this he was sure.

He had confidence in Emecheta and Renfrew. They would pull him through.

* * *

He felt a hand on his shoulder. Renfrew had turned to halt him. Ahead, Emecheta was crouching by a junction in the corridor, peering around the corner, laser poised.

Latimer heard his heart thudding, loud, in the confines of his EVA suit.

Emecheta stood and hurried back to them. They touched helmets. "Now I know why they haven't depressurised," he said. "Okay, we can crack our suits."

"You sure it's safe?" Renfrew asked.

"Sure I'm sure," Emecheta said, tapping the controls at the neck of his helmet. His faceplate whirred open and he breathed deeply.

Latimer cracked his helmet, tasting the fresh air and ... there was something else. An odour, at once sweet and rank.

"Em?" he asked. "What the hell ...?"

"Take a quick look around the corner, Ted. You'll see why they need air."

Heart slamming, fearing what he might find, but secretly knowing the answer, Latimer advanced cautiously towards the corner, paused and peered around.

89

The corridor opened out into a big chamber, featureless and grey.

Latimer ducked back and plastered himself against the wall, breathing hard. He had caught only a fleeting glimpse of the cyborged colonists in the distance. They had been cerebrally augmented, their crania implanted with leads and jacks that snaked down their backs and linked to what appeared to be powerpacks.

They were armed, and stood about in groups, casually, like soldiers awaiting a command.

He pulled back, breathing hard.

"Okay," Emecheta said. "What now?"

"Where's the emergency tube?" Latimer said.

Emecheta pointed. "Thataway – across the chamber."

"Great!" Renfrew hissed. Her teeth chattered in fright. "So … what do we do?"

"Well, we can't cross the corridor without those bastards seeing us," Emecheta said.

"There's got to be another tube nearby, right?" Latimer said.

Emecheta consulted the softscreen. "Here, to the left, about half a klick away." He indicated a corridor situated a short way behind them.

"Okay, let's go," Latimer said.

They hurried back the way they had come and turned down the corridor, almost running now in their haste to put as much distance as possible between themselves and the cyborgs.

It seemed to Latimer that every muscle in his body was straining in protest, his every joint in pain. After so long in cold sleep, he thought, what do I expect? His lungs burned, and every breath was an effort.

He heard a sound behind him – the distinctive snap of a laser's safety-catch – and turned.

A colonist crouched, raised a laser to his shoulder, taking aim. Still running, Latimer loosed off a volley of laser fire, filling the corridor with actinic glare. When his eyes adjusted, he saw the colonist in pieces on the deck. He ran on, gagging.

Beside him, Emecheta turned and laid down a continuous hail of laser fire. Latimer looked over his shoulder and saw more cyborged colonists appear. It's only a matter of time, he thought.

Lances of laser fire tore past him, superheating the air and ricocheting off the corridor ceiling, zigzagging crazily down the perspective of the receding passage. He ducked, screaming, and sprinted.

Then Emecheta was beside him again, pushing Latimer and Renfrew to their left, along another corridor.

Ahead, he made out the service hatch. He entered the code while Emecheta and Renfrew crouched at the turn in the corridor, halting the charge of the cyborgs.

When he had the hatch open, he called: "Okay! Move it!"

He climbed into the hatch and descended, aware of Renfrew and Emecheta crowding into the tube above him and closing the hatch.

Emecheta and Renfrew had paused in their descent. He halted also, listening.

He heard footsteps in the corridor, running past the hatch, and almost wept with relief.

Slowly, taking the utmost care not to make a sound, he began climbing down again.

Eleven

They might have been descending for an hour when Emecheta hissed down at him: "Okay, we're almost there. Let's stop and think this through."

Latimer halted, aware of his trembling limbs. He was exhausted, and realised that he'd been climbing on autopilot for who knew how long, his mind numbed with the import of past events, too afraid to look too far into the future.

He was grateful for the respite. He looked up at Renfrew and Emecheta.

"The hatch about three metres below you," Emecheta was saying, "gives on to a corridor ten metres from the entrance to the core. The cyborgs might not be in the corridor when we emerge, but you never know. We gotta be careful. You bet your bottom dollar that the bastards have Central well guarded."

"I don't see how we're going to do it," Latimer found himself saying.

"Fuck that!" Emecheta spat. "We go in there with all guns blazing. The element of surprise. Remember, all we gotta do is hit Central. Take my word for it, those cyborgs and the rest of the roboid horde, they ain't autonomous. They're slaved. We

92

hit Central, and the rest of the bastards go belly up."

Latimer nodded. "Okay, okay."

"Let's take a rest," Renfrew said. "I've about had it. I need a break."

"Fine," Emecheta said. "Take it easy. Deep breaths. Tell me when you're both ready to go, okay?"

Latimer let a silence develop, then said: "Anyone ever tell you, Em, you're a born leader?"

"That, coming from the boss!" Emecheta laughed.

"I knew what I was doing when things weren't mad crazy, Em."

Emecheta was smiling. "I never told you, did I?"

Latimer looked up. "What?"

"For two years back in my twenties, I fought for the Nigerian Liberation Front. Kept that off my CV when I applied for the colony mission."

Latimer said: "Thought you were pretty handy with that laser."

Renfrew, above him, laughed.

"What's with you?" Emecheta asked.

"I never thought I'd be in this position," she said. "I thought it would be all plain sailing once I'd been accepted. The colony programme. A new world. A new start. Exploration. Adventure ... but nothing like this."

A silence developed.

Renfrew went on: "What happened?"

Emecheta grunted. "What you mean, what happened?"

"I mean," she said, "why did the AIs turn on us, use us? I mean, whose fault is it?"

"It's no-one's fault, Serena," Emecheta said. "It just happened. Call it bad luck."

"The Omega Corporation programmed Central," Renfrew went on. "They had branches developing artificial intelligence, even cerebrally-assisted human-machine interfaces. They should have known that something like this might have happened, given the right circumstances."

Latimer said: "They weren't to know that! No-one could have predicted a thing like this. Like Em said, it's just bad luck. Period."

Renfrew made to reply, thought better of it, and let the silence stretch.

Emecheta ended it. "Okay, you two rested enough? Shall we continue?"

"Fine by me," Latimer said.

Renfrew nodded.

"Okay," Emecheta called down to Latimer. "Open the hatch slowly, take a look. If it's all clear, give us the thumbs up."

Latimer descended the last few metres. He entered the code in the control unit and opened the hatch with care.

He looked through, expecting to see the corridor crawling with cyborgs.

Instead it was still, silent.

He signalled to Renfrew and Emecheta and stepped through the hatch.

In the corridor, Emecheta studied the softscreen again. He pointed ahead. "This way. Ten metres, and then left. There's a big hatch. We have the code here." He indicated flashing alpha-numerics on the 'screen. "I expect the core'll be guarded, so as soon as we're through, begin firing, okay?"

Renfrew nodded, glancing at Latimer. He sensed her fear. He felt it himself. It should never have come to this, he thought. I don't belong here.

Emecheta was striding along the corridor. Latimer and Renfrew followed. They turned right, and came up against the triangular recessed entrance to the core.

While Emecheta tapped the code into the control unit,

94

Latimer and Renfrew readied their lasers.

Emecheta turned to them, shaking his head. "No luck."

"They've changed the code," Renfrew said. "They knew we were coming and changed the code."

The thought that the cyborg hordes were waiting beyond the hatch filled Latimer with dread.

"Okay," Emecheta said. "Stand back. I'll blast the unit open."

Renfrew said: "And tell them exactly where we are?"

"What about access tubes?" Latimer asked. "Let's check the softscreen, see if there's another way in there."

"This is the only way in, Ted," Emecheta said. "Don't you think I looked?"

They pored over the screen again. The core chamber that housed Central was a beehive-shaped well, surrounded by a series of rising circular galleries. A single entrance gave access to each level, with no access tubes or other means of entry.

They were outside the second lowest gallery. Latimer suspected that the cyborgs had stationed themselves on every level, awaiting their arrival. He wondered why they hadn't come out in search of them.

"So ..." Emecheta said. "What now?"

Renfrew looked at Latimer. The little of her face showing through her helmet looked white and petrified.

Latimer said: "Looks like our options are limited. Okay, blast the unit. But then we wait, okay? No heroics. Let's see what happens once the hatch is open."

Emecheta nodded. Latimer and Renfrew backed from the hatch, crouching in a recess in the corridor, while Emecheta stood beside them and aimed.

He fired. The glare was blinding. Latimer covered his eyes, and when he looked again the unit was a smouldering mass of melted circuitry and plastic.

The door stuttered open a metre and then stopped.

Latimer readied his laser, expecting an onslaught.

All was silent, suspiciously still.

He could see through the open hatch to the gallery beyond, and behind it the other galleries rising tier after tier.

There was no sign of the expected cyborg hordes.

He knew what they had to do now. In theory it was all very simple. Enter the well, lean over the gallery, and laser Central AI down below into a million pieces.

"Okay," Emecheta said. He glanced at Latimer and Renfrew, his face stern and beaded with perspiration. "I'll go first. I'll do what I can to destroy Central. I'll try to get in and out real fast. Get ready to back me up."

Latimer nodded.

Emecheta ran. He surged through the hatch like a quarterback, hit the gallery rail and fired. Immediately, fire was returned. A dozen lances of white light rained down from the galleries above. Emecheta ducked, rolled into a ball, and returned fire.

Without thinking, Latimer sprinted to the hatch, knelt, and sprayed laser fire high into the well of the chamber. He saw cyborgs explode in gouts of blood and metal, heard explosions and cries from throats that once had been human.

Emecheta was rolling, avoiding incoming fire, and loosing off shot after shot along the length of the gallery.

Latimer sighted to his left, along the curving gallery. Two cyborgs ran into view, lasers drawn. Latimer accounted for one, and Emecheta another: they hit the wall in sections, severed arms and legs spasming with ersatz life. Then Latimer saw that Renfrew was beside him, adding her fire-power to the battle.

For what seemed like an age, but must have been only

96

minutes, Latimer and Renfrew held their position by the hatch, repulsing the cyborgs as they emerged around the bend of the gallery and picking off the occasional sniper that showed its augmented head over the gallery rails above.

"It's no good," Emecheta called back. "We need to hit Central! I'm going over. Cover me!"

Before Latimer could protest, Emecheta hit the control of his power-pack and shot over the edge of the gallery. Latimer and Renfrew set up a constant volley of fire, filling the air with a whine of laser fire in a blinding blitz.

Emecheta disappeared from sight, and Latimer waited for the explosion that might signal the destruction of Central.

He waited, picking off cyborgs when they appeared, but no miraculous explosion came.

"Cover me!" he yelled at Renfrew. "I'm going in."

He darted, doubled up, through the hatch and hit the rail. While Renfrew covered him, and he loosed off shot after shot into the air, he stood and peered over the edge.

Down below, he made out the hexagonal hub that was Central AI, and beside it, his EVA suit neatly divided just below the waistline, the body of Emecheta. In the second it took to fully comprehend what had happened, Latimer saw that there were no living 'borgs down below. Before dying, Emecheta had accounted for a dozen or more of the monsters.

A shot fell from above, almost hitting him. He pushed himself from the rail and dived back through the hatch, pulling Renfrew after him.

"What?" she cried. "Where's Em?"

"This way," he told her. "Back to the tube."

They sprinted back along the corridor and piled into the access tube, Latimer dogging the hatch behind him.

"Ted?" Renfrew pleaded. "What happened?"

"Em's dead," he said, the words catching in his throat like

a bolus of phlegm. "We're going down, to the lowest level."

"And then?"

"It's hardly protected. Em killed a whole bunch of the bastards. If we blast the hatch we can blow Central to hell."

Without waiting for her to respond, he began climbing down. His breath came in rasping spasms, his heart thumping. He felt dizzy, nauseous, and had to concentrate to keep himself moving. How easy it would be to stop and rest.

When he came to the hatch, he paused and listened. There was not a sound from outside.

He imagined the cyborgs taking stock of their casualties, regrouping, trying to second-guess his and Renfrew's next line of attack.

He cracked the hatch and peered out. The corridor was deserted. He signalled Renfrew to follow him, and slipped from the tube.

He ran along the corridor and crouched at the corner. Ahead, he made out the triangular entrance to the core.

Panting, Renfrew dropped into a crouch beside him, laser at the ready.

He was about to blast the control unit when the communicator on the sleeve of his arms chimed, and the miniature screen flared into life.

Startled, he lifted his arm and stared at the face on the screen.

"Ted," a familiar voice said, "we need to talk. If you join us ..."

She went on, but Latimer no longer heard the words. He was staring down at the perfect face of his wife. Carrie seemed unmarked by the depredations visited upon the rest of the colonists. Her face was as he recalled it: serene and oval, for all the world like a ballerina's.

"You should not resist what you do not understand, Ted.

Join us, and apprehend the wonder of what we will achieve."

Beside him, Renfrew reached out and killed the screen.

"They'll be homing in on the signal!" she said. "Come on, move it!"

They ran, and then came to a sudden halt as a figure appeared around the corner.

Carrie faced them, small and graceful, smiling at them with one hand outstretched. "Ted, please. This is ridiculous. If you join us, we can be together ..."

He felt himself weaken. He wanted to reach out to her, take his wife in his arms. The sight of her brought back so many memories and associations that, for a second, it was easy to forget where he was.

She was perfect, undamaged, and yet he knew that she must be like all the others.

She was perfect – except, he saw, she no longer wore her blonde fall of hair long and around her shoulders: her skull was shaven.

And only then did he make out the silver spars and jacks implanted in her cranium.

"Ted, join me ..."

He gripped his laser. "And become like you?" he said through his tears.

She smiled. "I am better, Ted. Improved. Please believe me."

"Improved? You ... you were perfect. You've become a monster, like the rest of them. What they did to the other colonists –"

"That was a necessary part of the process, Ted. We had to learn. We had to make mistakes before we learned how to achieve union. What happened was inevitable, a process of evolution."

He stared at her. "What do you mean?"

99

"Scientists foresaw it," she said. "Even back then." She smiled at him, and he recalled all the other times she had smiled like that, and before she could go on, tell him what he did not want to hear, he raised his laser.

But he couldn't bring himself to fire.

"Do it!" Renfrew hissed beside him.

He choked on a sob as Caroline smiled, reached out for him.

"Then I will!" Renfrew said, and raised her own laser.

Latimer heard the blast, and Caroline's gasp, but closed his eyes to spare himself.

Then he felt Renfrew's gloved hand grip his. "Come on! This way. They know where we are!"

He was running, blindly, obeying the dictates of some innate survival mechanism.

They turned a corner and Renfrew stabbed at a control unit beside a sliding door. They passed into a padded chamber and halted, panting.

They were in an observation nacelle, a semi-circular blister that obtruded through the skin of the ship. Curved rectangular viewscreens looked out into space, a depth of velvet blackness decorated by a million scintillating stars.

Beside him, Renfrew was laughing, hysterically. She fell against the closed hatch and laughed until she wept.

Latimer felt himself losing control. He thought of Carrie, and wondered if it was better now that she was dead and no longer suffering.

But had she suffered? Perhaps she had been, as she claimed, improved? The thought filled him with dread.

Renfrew had slid into a crouch against the hatch, still laughing.

"What?" Latimer said.

"Ted, think about it! Those cyborgs out there! Think about

it! The reason they didn't depressurise the ship was because the cyborgs had to breathe, right?"

"My God ..."

"Right on, Ted. We can beat the bastards! Seal your suit then get back into the corridor."

He lowered his faceplate and sealed his helmet. In seconds he was breathing canned air in eerie silence.

They stepped through the hatch, back into the corridor, and Renfrew stood foursquare before the sliding door and ordered Latimer to close the hatch. "Then hold on tight, Ted!"

She had it all planned, he thought. He hit the control panel.

Behind them, along the corridor, he heard the sound of running feet. He swung round and fired, and the first phalanx of cyborgs came up against his shots. They fell, screaming.

Behind them, others appeared.

"Serena!" Latimer yelled.

The sliding door closed on the muzzle of her laser, and she fired.

In the nacelle, the viewscreen shattered. Latimer heard nothing, but felt the force of the displaced air as it tore past him, smacking Renfrew against the partially closed hatch.

Along the corridor, cyborgs fell to their knees, gagging. He watched, at once appalled and fascinated, as their flesh turned blue, exploded.

Seconds later, the pressure equalised, Latimer and Renfrew hurried along the corridor, dodging corpses, and stopped before the triangular hatch to the core.

Renfrew blasted the control unit and the hatch jerked open. Whatever had been alive and breathing in there, Latimer knew, was no longer.

Ahead, beyond a grotesque tableau of asphyxiated

101

cyborgs, piled alongside those that Emecheta had killed, was the hexagonal hub of Central AI.

Beyond it were the halved pieces of Em's EVA suit. He had been so close, Latimer thought.

Smiling to himself, filled with a bitter sense of satisfaction mingling with the pain, Latimer raised his laser.

Beside him, Renfrew did the same.

For a second, the screen set into the console above the banked terminal pulsed with a pattern of Mandelbrot fractals, and Latimer wondered if Central was about to plead for its life.

He signalled to Renfrew. Together they burned the AI, and stopped only when Central was a blackened, smouldering pile of slag.

Twelve

They made their way back up though the shattered nose-section of the ship, passing dead cyborgs and malfunctioning machine intelligences on the way. They depressurised the sealed sections of the ship as they went by the simple expedient of blasting open hatches and doors with their lasers. They were cautious, lest rogue cyborgs had had time to locate EVA suits and save themselves.

They came across little resistance, one trilobite drone stuck in a cycle of endlessly firing off its laser pistol, and a cyborg that was dead, but slaved to an exoskeleton programmed to fire its laser at selected targets: in this case, EVA suits. Renfrew accounted for the trilobite, but Latimer almost walked into the slaved cyborg before raising his laser and slicing it to pieces.

They came to the impact breach torn through the ship, and powered themselves circumspectly through the vacuum. It would be tragic, Latimer thought, to come this far only to slip up through complacency.

They made the other side and rode an upchute to the command unit.

Latimer cracked open his helmet and held Renfrew as she wept.

* * *

They sat at their com-stations and regarded the scene through the viewscreen.

Hangar Two hung against a backdrop of stars, drifting.

"That's our only hope, Serena," he said. "If the AIs didn't get to them ..."

She turned to him. "And the mission? How do we get the ship back on course, without Central? How do we find a suitable colony world? I'm no com-expert, Ted."

He smiled at her. "Think about it. There are bound to be com-experts in hangar Two –"

"If," Renfrew said, "they're still alive."

He stared out at the drifting hangar. "I know they are," he said. He was convinced. There were a thousand colonists out there, totally oblivious to the horror that had ensued while they slept.

The alternative, that they were dead, or that the AIs had got to them, was unthinkable.

The two of them, alone on a crippled starship ...

He stood up, affixed his helmet. "Okay, let's go take a look, shall we?"

They pressurised their suits and cycled themselves through the airlock. *Déjà-vu*, Latimer thought, as he attached the safety cable and activated his powerpack. It seemed such a long time ago that he had last passed this way with Emecheta.

They exchanged a glance and kicked off, floating high above the wreckage of the superstructure. Minutes later, they approached the great ugly bulk of the disconnected hangar.

Latimer reached out and grabbed a hank of cable, and seconds later Renfrew joined him. They hung side by side, like swimmers enjoying a break at the side of the pool.

Latimer examined the twisted power supply and air leads. He opened up radio communications with Renfrew. "They seem intact and undamaged, Serena. Let's hope the sleepers weren't too shook up in the blast."

"They'll be fine, Ted," she murmured.

Hand over hand, Latimer hauled himself along the length of the cable towards the big bull's eye on the door of the emergency exit. They floated side by side, Latimer hesitating before keying in the code that would open the air-lock.

They had brought their lasers along, just in case. With his free hand he unclipped his.

"We won't be needing them, Ted," Renfrew reassured him.

"Hope you're right ..." he said. He unclipped the safety cable from his suit and attached it to the lug beside the entrance, then punched in the code.

The air lock door slid open; lights winked on within. They jumped into the lock and the door closed behind them. Half a minute later, the inner door cycled open and Latimer floated through. He was aware that beside him, despite her optimism, Renfrew had levelled her laser. He found the control panel and activated the halogens, and seconds later the chamber was flooded with light.

He found himself weeping with relief. There were no hostile cyborgs or roboids to greet them, no scene of wholesale butchery. The hangar was as it should be: row after row of cold sleep pods, their covers shut, their running lights sequencing normally.

They powered up and jetted over the gallery. Latimer directed himself down between the first rows of pods and floated towards the nearest. He looked through the crystal cover and felt tears coursing down his cheeks.

A young Asian woman lay fast asleep, her face serene. He bobbed along to the next pod, this one occupied by a European in his thirties.

He heard Renfrew's small voice in his helmet: "They're okay, Ted. Christ, they're okay. Every one of them!"

He turned. She was floating beside a com console set into the bulkhead at the end of the row. Latimer jetted over to her and examined the scrolling diagnostics.

"One hundred percent survival rate as of now," she reported, a catch in her voice. "Absolutely no problems at all ..."

If only this had been Carrie's hangar, Latimer found himself thinking.

He said: "Access the files. Let's see what specialisms we have here."

With a clumsy, gloved finger, Renfrew tapped the touch-pad.

The manifest flashed up. She entered a command to find a com-expert among the sleeping colonists.

A second later the message appeared: *None Found.*

Renfrew laughed. "Christ, Ted ..." She was scrolling down the list of a thousand names. "We've got agriculturists and biologists and zoologists ... all the soft sciences, but not one damned computer specialist."

He felt his elation quickly turn to something very much like despair. "So ... what now?"

A beat, then Renfrew said: "Let's get back to the command unit. We'll try to assess the extent of the damage, see what we can rig up ..."

A cold weight lodged in his chest, Latimer nodded and followed Renfrew towards the air-lock. They cycled themselves through, attached the safety cables, and powered themselves back towards the distant, tiny light of the emergency exit high on the side of the command unit.

They had come so far, Latimer told himself, overcome such extreme odds, that they would not be defeated now. They would manage somehow to find a habitable, Earth-like world.

He wondered if he was deluding himself. It would be a tragedy if, after everything they had experienced in the past few days, they were to spend the rest of their lives wallowing at sub-lightspeed between the stars. He could not bring himself to accept the enormity of the idea.

They reached the emergency exit and cycled themselves through, into the welcome familiarity of the command unit.

Latimer broke the seal on his helmet, pulled it off and dropped his laser.

Beside him, something about Renfrew's body language alerted him. She had stopped, stiffened, and was staring across the unit towards the com-stations.

He followed her gaze.

Someone was sitting before the consoles, facing them.

It was Jenny Li.

Thirteen

Latimer's first thought was that it was a mistake to have cast aside his laser – the second, that Jenny Li, or whatever she had become, was not armed.

She sat in the swivel-chair, in her EVA suit, having removed the helmet. She looked tiny within the bulky suit, even smaller somehow because of her shaven skull.

She smiled across at them. "Don't be afraid Serena, Ted," she said. "It's okay. I won't harm you."

Renfrew stared at her. "How ... how the hell did you survive?"

Jenny Li shrugged the massive shoulders of her EVA suit. "I was the only augmented human in the theatre when you depressurised the ship. All the others had been sent to capture you. When I realised what you'd done, I suited up and made my way back here."

Renfrew shook her head. "I mean ... earlier. I thought ... Emecheta was supposed to have ..."

Then Latimer knew why Jenny Li was still alive: Emecheta had shot her, but the AI surgeons had repaired her, brought her back to life: it was not, after all, that much of a miracle, considering what they had done to the other sleepers.

Her high laughter filled the unit. She said: "Oh, Em couldn't bring himself to end my suffering, Serena."

Renfrew said: "Emecheta didn't ...?"

"I saw him return," Jenny Li said. "I was conscious all the time, you know. All the time they were cutting me. I couldn't feel a thing – but I knew exactly what they were doing to me. Anyway, I saw you up there. At first I hoped you'd be able to do something, rescue me. But I knew that was impossible. Then Em came back, and I knew why. I saw him aim the pistol, and I willed him to kill me ... but he couldn't bring himself to do it."

Latimer considered the big Nigerian, then, his cold rationality ... So he had had a fallible, human side, after all. He wondered if that was why Emecheta had sacrificed himself in the end, because he knew that his inability to kill Jenny Li had compromised their mission to destroy Central?

"Me and Em," Jenny went on, "we were close, once. Then Em just turned off, concentrated wholly on the mission, ignored me." She smiled. "But in the end, his humanity won out – he couldn't kill me."

Latimer shook his head. "None of us could. We ... we wanted to – for your sake as well as ours. We didn't want you telling the AIs what we'd planned."

Jenny Li smiled. "Oh, how I cursed Em when he didn't pull the trigger! But then, a minute later, I realised how fortunate I was that he hadn't. The AIs gave me something wonderful, you know."

Renfrew said: "They turned you into a machine!"

But Li was shaking her head. "They turned me into something that retained my humanity, but also gave me something much more."

Latimer thought of Carrie, and did not want to hear what Jenny Li was telling him.

She went on: "I was still me, still human, but I had access to such knowledge, such a wealth of understanding."

"And now?" Renfrew asked.

"The same," Li said. "Oh, because Central is destroyed, the cache of knowledge available is reduced. But, in here," and she raised a small hand to the input jacks at the base of her skull, "in here, I have a much greater understanding ... of everything."

Latimer said: "We had to destroy Central, Jenny–"

She smiled, interrupting him. "No, Ted. You *thought* you had to destroy Central. Based on the knowledge available to you, by your own criteria, you had to do as you did. But your knowledge was partial; you acted on ignorance."

"We wanted to survive," Latimer said, "as we were."

"But you didn't even know what it was, truly, we wanted to change you into."

Renfrew stepped forward. She found a swivel-chair and slumped into it. "Central," she said, holding her head. She looked up, at Jenny Li. "Central was undamaged when we reached it."

The diminutive Korean smiled.

Latimer said: "I don't understand."

Renfrew turned to him. "Don't you see? Central was undamaged. We assumed, all along, that it was damage to Central that had sent it crazy, made it turn against us." She faced Jenny Li and said in a whisper: "But it was planned all along, wasn't it?"

Jenny Li shook her head. "Not at all. Just as the human crew was given directives, so was Central. Its directive was to survive at all costs, and to ensure the survival of the colonists. It deemed that, in the interests of the mission, a union should take place."

"So when the ship hit the cometary storm–" Renfrew began.

110

"There was no storm," the Korean said.

Latimer said: "The Hansen-Spirek coils … The Earth First activist was right."

"The probes," Renfrew said. "My God, the Omega Corporation knew they were sending us out with defective drives."

Jenny Li said: "They knew there was a sixty percent chance that the coils would malfunction – but the Corporation had already invested so much, and Earth was so near crisis point, that they deemed it necessary to go ahead with the mission." She paused, then went on. "In the event, they were correct. We *had* to leave Earth, whatever the potential risk."

Latimer said: "What do you mean?" He had an awful feeling that he knew very well what she meant.

She sighed. "Central received two communiqués from Earth, one twenty years after we set off, the second after thirty years. We couldn't access them up here, of course."

Renfrew said: "And? What did Earth say?"

"The first message," Li said, "reported a war on Earth between Europe and Oceana, biological plagues, mass slaughter. It was estimated that some two billion human beings perished in the war and its aftermath."

"Christ," Latimer said, finding a seat and slumping into it. And he thought he had experienced the ultimate horror aboard the *Dauntless*.

He thought of his sister, her kids. What chance that they had survived? Then he realised that this was all ancient history, now.

Renfrew said: "And the communiqué after thirty years?"

The Korean shook her shaven head. "It was little more than a farewell message, put together by a few surviving scientists. The war had continued, turning nuclear. Earth was moving into a self-induced ice age; they forecast that all life

111

on Earth would be extinct within twenty-five years."

The enormity of the concept, allied to the idea that all this had happened hundreds of years ago, turned the tragedy into something abstract. It would be a long while before he fully understood what Jenny Li had told him.

Renfrew sat up: "So ... we're the survivors, Jenny. You and me and Ted and the thousand colonists. We're all that remain ..."

Latimer said: "What now? Is there any hope of finding a suitable planet?"

He saw something then in Jenny Li's eyes – perhaps the desire to tell him that, if they had spared Central, then the chances would have been excellent. He wondered what it was that had stopped Jenny reminding him of what they had done in destroying Central – the machine part of her, or the human?

She said: "While you were across at hangar Two, I patched together a rough com system. With what I have up here," – she touched her head – "and the unit's auxiliary system I've repaired, we have a matrix that should be able to detect a habitable planet. Of course, we'll be moving at well below maximum speed, so it might take that much longer. But the computers servicing the cold sleep system are working AOK, so we should last the journey."

A silence opened up between them. At last Latimer said: "And you're on our side, Jenny?"

She smiled. "Whatever I might have become, Ted, I'm still human. I want to survive, with my species. Of course I'm on your side."

Later, they prepared themselves for another period of cold sleep. Jenny Li told them that she had instructed the com-system to wake them in fifteen hundred years, for maintenance checks, or before that if they should happen upon a suitable, Earth-like planet.

As Latimer stretched out and gave himself to the crawling sub-dermal capillaries, his last thought was whether it was wise to have trusted her.

* * *

He woke slowly. His first thought was of Carrie, and of what had happened to her. Then he remembered the thousand surviving colonists, and finding Jenny Li in the command unit ...

He peered at the digital display above his head. Jenny had set the chronometers to zero before they slept – and now his read 800.

Which meant they had emerged before the fifteen hundred years scheduled for a maintenance check.

Which, he reasoned, could mean only they had come across a planet.

Either that, or there was another emergency.

He sat up. Renfrew emerged from her pod opposite Latimer. She smiled at him. "Was all that a dream, Ted?"

"A nightmare, Serena. But it happened." He pointed across the unit, to where an augmented Jenny Li sat at her com-station. "There's the proof."

Across the chamber, Li swivelled in her chair.

"What's happening?" Latimer asked. He stood, unsteadily, and crossed the unit to his own com-station. Renfrew followed him.

"What were you expecting?" Li asked, smiling. "Another Hansen-Spirek blow-out?"

"After what happened last time," Renfrew said, "I'm ready for anything."

Jenny Li tipped back her head and laughed, and the gesture was so human that Latimer could almost ignore the

113

sight of the ugly cranial augmentation that adhered to the base of her skull. "Are you ready even," she said, "for a virgin, Earth-type world, ninety-eight percent Earth-norm gravity, breathable oxygen-nitrogen atmosphere, no indigenous sentient lifeforms …? In other words, the perfect colony world."

Something like elation swelled in Latimer's chest. "You're joking, right?"

"No joke," Jenny Li said, swivelling in her seat and hitting the touch-pad. "Alkaid VII, as yet unnamed."

Above her, the viewscreen flared with a panoramic view of a mountainous valley falling away to a plain of blue-green grass and strange, attenuated trees.

"I sent a few probes down as soon as I came round. It looks like paradise, Ted."

She tapped the touch-pad, and the scene on the viewscreen changed. Now they stared at a coastal landscape, a scimitar beach backed by rolling blue-green hills. Latimer made out lumbering, pachydermal beasts, snuffling through the red sands.

"I repaired the com-system linking the unit with hangar Two," Li went on. "The sleepers are all doing fine."

"What about the shuttles?" Latimer asked, aware that if they had been destroyed in the accident, then there would be no way of reaching the surface of the new world.

"I've checked. Three of the six were destroyed when the coil exploded. But the three others are in good working order. I've put the *Dauntless* into a low orbit. We can start waking the colonists, getting them down to the shuttle hangar."

When she stopped talking, a silence developed. Suddenly Latimer laughed, and instinctively reached out and pulled Renfrew and Li towards him.

114

Coda

He was awoken early by a gorgeous orange sunrise in the west. He slipped out of bed, dressed and left the dome.

He stood in the warm morning light, stretching and inhaling the heavy scent of the flowering shrubs that grew in the garden surrounding the dome.

Down in the valley, another day was beginning: domes were being constructed, roads laid, fields tilled.

A year since landfall, the colonisation of Arcadia was progressing according to schedule. The society would have been better equipped, and balanced, if the four thousand sleepers had not perished aboard the *Dauntless*, but the one thousand and three surviving colonists would provide a sufficiently varied gene pool in order for a viable colony to prosper.

And Arcadia had proved a welcoming world, with few vicious predators – animal or viral – to worry the colonists. They had settled a clement equatorial region, with hot summers and mild winters, and set up farms, a few outlying villages and this, Latimer's hometown, Landfall City, home to some six hundred souls, and rising.

Latimer worked as an engineer in Landfall, supervising

the slow expansion. At nights, he sat at his com-screen and slowly wrote out the story of what had happened aboard the *Dauntless*.

Sometimes, when daunted by the prospect of accurately setting it all down, when the emotions brought about by the memories became too much, he would leave the dome and stroll up the hillside, sit on the blue-green grass and stare up at the star-packed sky.

Sol was a tiny speck of light high in the northern sky, but it was hard to associate the star with the cradle of humankind. The first children were being born on Arcadia, and soon they would learn all about the troubled history of planet Earth.

That had been something Latimer had worried over during the long months of establishing the colony: how to shape a society that would not fall into the traps that had brought life on Earth to its knees.

It was a conundrum beyond his limited knowledge: the future, he knew, was unknowable; he could but trust in the goodness of the individuals around him to perpetuate a fair and equable society, based on equality and tolerance.

He spent long hours wondering if what he had done with Renfrew, in the core of the *Dauntless*, had been the right thing. At the time, of course, fighting for his life, there had been no other course of action. But every time he beheld the diminutive figure of Jenny Li, every time he interacted with the obviously caring and compassionate human being she had become, he questioned his actions ... and wondered at a future that would have contained Caroline.

Now he sat on the bench before his dome and watched three small figures leave the ground-effect vehicle on the road far below, and begin the long climb towards him. They were Renfrew, Li, and a biologist called Freya Sinclair, whose

116

friendship for the past month had diverted his thoughts from what might have been.

Together, he and these three constituted the steering committee of the Landfall Anniversary Celebrations, to be held the following week.

Smiling, aware of his good fortune, Latimer stood and strolled down the hillside to greet his friends.

About The Author

Eric Brown has written over twenty books and eighty short stories in the SF genre. He has twice won the BSFA short story award, in 2000 and 2002. His first collection was *The Time-Lapsed Man* (1990), and he has recently sold his sixth, *Threshold Shift*, due out from Golden Gryphon in the US. His first novel was *Meridian Days* (1992). The third book of the Virex trilogy, *New York Dreams*, appeared in 2004, as did his novel *Bengal Station*. Forthcoming books include *The Fall of Tartarus* and *The Extraordinary Voyage of Jules Verne*. His website can be found at: http://ericbrownsf.port5.com/

Other Telos Titles Available

TIME HUNTER

A range of high-quality, original paperback and limited edition hardback novellas featuring the adventures in time of Honoré Lechasseur. Part mystery, part detective story, part dark fantasy, part science fiction ... these books are guaranteed to enthral fans of good fiction everywhere, and are in the spirit of our acclaimed range of *Doctor Who* Novellas.

ALREADY AVAILABLE

THE WINNING SIDE
by LANCE PARKIN
Emily is dead! Killed by an unknown assailant. Honoré and Emily find themselves caught up in a plot reaching from the future to their past, and with their very existence, not to mention the future of the entire world, at stake, can they unravel the mystery before it is too late?
An adventure in time and space.
£7.99 (+ £1.50 UK p&p) Standard p/b ISBN 1-903889-35-9 (pb)
£25.00 (+ £1.50 UK p&p) Deluxe h/b ISBN 1-903889-36-7 (hb)

THE TUNNEL AT THE END OF THE LIGHT
by STEFAN PETRUCHA
In the heart of post-war London, a bomb is discovered lodged at a disused station between Green Park and Hyde Park Corner. The bomb detonates, and as the dust clears, it becomes apparent that *something* has been awakened. Strange half-human creatures attack the workers at the site, hungrily searching for anything containing sugar ...

Meanwhile, Honoré and Emily are contacted by eccentric poet Randolph Crest, who believes himself to be the target of these subterranean creatures. The ensuing investigation brings Honoré and Emily up against a terrifying force from deep beneath the earth, and one which even with their combined powers, they may have trouble stopping.

An adventure in time and space.

£7.99 (+ £1.50 UK p&p) Standard p/b ISBN 1-903889-37-5 (pb)
£25.00 (+ £1.50 UK p&p) Deluxe h/b ISBN 1-903889-38-3 (hb)

THE CLOCKWORK WOMAN
by CLAIRE BOTT
Honoré and Emily find themselves imprisoned in the 19th Century by a celebrated inventor ... but help comes from an unexpected source – a humanoid automaton created by and to give pleasure to its owner. As the trio escape to London, they are unprepared for what awaits them, and at every turn it seems impossible to avert what fate may have in store for the Clockwork Woman.

An adventure in time and space.

£7.99 (+ £1.50 UK p&p) Standard p/b ISBN 1-903889-39-1 (pb)
£25.00 (+ £1.50 UK p&p) Deluxe h/b ISBN 1-903889-40-5 (hb)

KITSUNE
by JOHN PAUL CATTON
In the year 2020, Honoré and Emily find themselves thrown
into a mystery, as an ice spirit – *Yuki-Onna* – wreaks havoc
during the Kyoto Festival, and a haunted funhouse proves to
contain more than just paper lanterns and wax dummies. But
what does all this have to do with the elegant owner of the
Hide and Chic fashion chain … and to the legendary Chinese
fox-spirits, the Kitsune?
An adventure in time and space.
£7.99 (+ £1.50 UK p&p) Standard p/b ISBN 1-903889-41-3 (pb)
£25.00 (+ £1.50 UK p&p) Deluxe h/b ISBN 1-903889-42-1 (hb)

THE SEVERED MAN
by GEORGE MANN
What links a clutch of sinister murders in Victorian London,
an angel appearing in a Staffordshire village in the 1920s and
a small boy running loose around the capital in 1950? When
Honoré and Emily encounter a man who appears to have been
cut out of time, they think they have the answer. But soon
enough they discover that the mystery is only just beginning
and that nightmares can turn into reality.
An adventure in time and space.
£7.99 (+ £1.50 UK p&p) Standard p/b ISBN 1-903889-43-X (pb)
£25.00 (+ £1.50 UK p&p) Deluxe h/b ISBN 1-903889-44-8 (hb)

TIME HUNTER FILM

DAEMOS RISING
by DAVID J HOWE, DIRECTED BY KEITH BARNFATHER
Daemos Rising is a sequel to both the *Doctor Who* adventure *The Daemons* and to *Downtime*, an earlier drama featuring the Yeti. It is also a prequel of sorts to Telos Publishing's *Time Hunter* series. It stars Miles Richardson as ex-UNIT operative Douglas Cavendish, and Beverley Cressman as Brigadier Lethbridge-Stewart's daughter Kate. Trapped in an isolated cottage, Cavendish thinks he is seeing ghosts. The only person who might understand and help is Kate Lethbridge-Stewart ... but when she arrives, she realises that Cavendish is key in a plot to summon the Daemons back to the Earth. With time running out, Kate discovers that sometimes even the familiar can turn out to be your worst nightmare. Also starring Andrew Wisher, and featuring Ian Richardson as the Narrator.
An adventure in time and space.
£14.00 (+ £2.50 UK p&p) PAL format R4 DVD
Order direct from Reeltime Pictures, PO Box 23435, London SE26 5WU

HORROR/FANTASY

CAPE WRATH by PAUL FINCH
Death and horror on a deserted Scottish island as an ancient
Viking warrior chief returns to life.
£8.00 (+ £1.50 UK p&p) Standard p/b ISBN: 1-903889-60-X

KING OF ALL THE DEAD
by STEVE LOCKLEY & PAUL LEWIS
The king of all the dead will have what is his.
£8.00 (+ £1.50 UK p&p) Standard p/b ISBN: 1-903889-61-8

GUARDIAN ANGEL by STEPHANIE BEDWELL-GRIME
Devilish fun as Guardian Angel Porsche Winter loses a soul to
the devil …
£9.99 (+ £2.50 UK p&p) Standard p/b ISBN: 1-903889-62-6

FALLEN ANGEL by STEPHANIE BEDWELL-GRIME
Porsche Winter battles she devils on Earth …
£9.99 (+ £2.50 UK p&p) Standard p/b ISBN: 1-903889-69-3

ASPECTS OF A PSYCHOPATH by ALISTAIR LANGSTON
Goes deeper than ever before into the twisted psyche of a
serial killer. Horrific, graphic and gripping, this book is not
for the squeamish.
£8.00 (+ £1.50 UK p&p) Standard p/b ISBN: 1-903889-63-4

SPECTRE by STEPHEN LAWS
The inseparable Byker Chapter: six boys, one girl, growing up together in the back streets of Newcastle. Now memories are all that Richard Eden has left, and one treasured photograph. But suddenly, inexplicably, the images of his companions start to fade, and as they vanish, so his friends are found dead and mutilated. Something is stalking the Chapter, picking them off one by one, something connected with their past, and with the girl they used to know.
£9.99 (+ £2.50 UK p&p) Standard p/b ISBN: 1-903889-72-3

THE HUMAN ABSTRACT by GEORGE MANN
A future tale of private detectives, AIs, Nanobots, love and death.
£7.99 (+ £1.50 UK p&p) Standard p/b ISBN: 1-903889-65-0

BREATHE by CHRISTOPHER FOWLER
The Office meets *Night of the Living Dead.*
£7.99 (+ £1.50 UK p&p) Standard p/b ISBN: 1-903889-67-7
£25.00 (+ £1.50 UK p&p) Deluxe h/b ISBN: 1-903889-68-5

HOUDINI'S LAST ILLUSION by STEVE SAVILE
Can the master illusionist Harry Houdini outwit the dead shades of his past?
£7.99 (+ £1.50 UK p&p) Standard p/b ISBN: 1-903889-66-9

ALICE'S JOURNEY BEYOND THE MOON by R J CARTER
A sequel to the classic Lewis Carroll tales.
£6.99 (+ £1.50 UK p&p) Standard p/b ISBN: 1-903889-76-6
£30.00 (+ £1.50 UK p&p) Deluxe h/b ISBN: 1-903889-77-4

TV/FILM GUIDES

A DAY IN THE LIFE: THE UNOFFICIAL AND
UNAUTHORISED GUIDE TO 24 by KEITH TOPPING
Complete episode guide to the first season of the popular TV show.
£9.99 (+ £2.50 p&p) Standard p/b ISBN: 1-903889-53-7

THE TELEVISION COMPANION: THE UNOFFICIAL
AND UNAUTHORISED GUIDE TO DOCTOR WHO by
DAVID J HOWE & STEPHEN JAMES WALKER
Complete episode guide to the popular TV show.
£14.99 (+ £4.75 UK p&p) Standard p/b ISBN: 1-903889-51-0

LIBERATION: THE UNOFFICIAL AND
UNAUTHORISED GUIDE TO BLAKE'S 7 by ALAN
STEVENS & FIONA MOORE
Complete episode guide to the popular TV show.
Featuring a foreword by David Maloney
£9.99 (+ £2.50 UK p&p) Standard p/b ISBN: 1-903889-54-5

HOWE'S TRANSCENDENTAL TOYBOX: SECOND
EDITION by DAVID J HOWE & ARNOLD T BLUMBERG
Complete guide to *Doctor Who* Merchandise.
£25.00 (+ £4.75 UK p&p) Standard p/b ISBN: 1-903889-56-1

HOWE'S TRANSCENDENTAL TOYBOX: UPDATE No.
1: 2003 by DAVID J HOWE & ARNOLD T BLUMBERG
Guide to *Doctor Who* Merchandise released in 2003.
£7.99 (+ £1.50 UK p&p) Standard p/b ISBN: 1-903889-57-X

A VAULT OF HORROR by KEITH TOPPING
A Guide to 80 Classic (and not so classic) British Horror Films
£12.99 (+ £4.75 UK p&p) Standard p/b ISBN: 1-903889-58-8

HANK JANSON

Classic pulp crime thrillers from the 1940s and 1950s.

TORMENT by HANK JANSON
£9.99 (+ £1.50 UK p&p) Standard p/b ISBN: 1-903889-80-4
WOMEN HATE TILL DEATH by HANK JANSON
£9.99 (+ £1.50 UK p&p) Standard p/b ISBN: 1-903889-81-2
SOME LOOK BETTER DEAD by HANK JANSON
£9.99 (+ £1.50 UK p&p) Standard p/b ISBN: 1-903889-82-0
SKIRTS BRING ME SORROW by HANK JANSON
£9.99 (+ £1.50 UK p&p) Standard p/b ISBN: 1-903889-83-9
WHEN DAMES GET TOUGH by HANK JANSON
£9.99 (+ £1.50 UK p&p) Standard p/b ISBN: 1-903889-85-5
ACCUSED by HANK JANSON
£9.99 (+ £1.50 UK p&p) Standard p/b ISBN: 1-903889-86-3
KILLER by HANK JANSON
£9.99 (+ £1.50 UK p&p) Standard p/b ISBN: 1-903889-87-1
FRAILS CAN BE SO TOUGH by HANK JANSON
£9.99 (+ £1.50 UK p&p) Standard p/b ISBN: 1-903889-88-X

Non-fiction

THE TRIALS OF HANK JANSON by STEVE HOLLAND
£12.99 (+ £2.50 UK p&p) Standard p/b ISBN: 1-903889-84-7

The prices shown are correct at time of going to press. However, the publishers reserve the right to increase prices from those previously advertised without prior notice.

TELOS PUBLISHING
c/o Beech House, Chapel Lane, Moulton, Cheshire, CW9
8PQ, England
Email: orders@telos.co.uk
Web: www.telos.co.uk

To order copies of any Telos books, please visit our website where there are full details of all titles and facilities for worldwide credit card online ordering, or send a cheque or postal order (UK only) for the appropriate amount (including postage and packing), together with details of the book(s) you require, plus your name and address to the above address. Overseas readers please send two international reply coupons for details of prices and postage rates.